Sophie Parkin's main ambition in life is to have as much fun as humanly possible. This has manifested itself in many ways throughout the years. As a rug rat it was making mud and worm pies, and as she got older she maintained her interest in cooking but added chatting and climbing trees to her array of abilities as a seasoned tomboy.

Sophie has a degree in Fine Art, otherwise known as painting, chatting, writing and partying. In between chatting, she has had two children (Paris and Carson), has had painting exhibitions, run nightclubs, written grown-up novels and for newspapers, been a kids' Agony Aunt for AOL and cooked quite a lot. She has no pets or husbands as she might be allergic to both – except for a stray cat called Cat, who loves her only for her copious gifts of milk and salmon. It is a simple one-way relationship.

This is her third teenage novel. Unlike Lily, Sophie has never passed a French exam, and has never learned to speak another language. However she does love Paris (her son and the city) and is very fond of berets and most French food that doesn't involve cows', sheep's or pigs' intestines.

Bazaar Nights and Camel Bites

the life and loves of lily

Sophie Parkin

Piccadilly Press • London

To Zulieka and Papa who taught me to love Tangier

First published in Great Britain in 2007
by Piccadilly Press Ltd,
5 Castle Road, London NW1 8PR
www.piccadillypress.co.uk

A catalogue record for this book is available
from the British Library

ISBN-13: 978 1 85340 939 4 (trade paperback)

1 3 5 7 9 10 8 6 4 2

Printed in the UK by CPI Bookmarque, Croydon, CR0 4TD
Text design by Textype, Cambridge
Cover design by Susan Hellard and Simon Davis
Set in Dom Casual and ITC Legacy

CHAPTER ONE
Joyeux Noël

24th December – Polka-dot Pants

'Don't be so stupid, Lily. You can't buy her those!'

'Why not?'

'Because you're not supposed to buy grown-ups knickers. It's rude and what would your father say?'

'He's your father too, or are you trying to pretend you're not my sister again? Anyway, they're not rude – they're funny. I mean, who wouldn't want a pair of scarlet knickers with a giant polka-dot bow on the bum for Christmas, or any other time of year? Suzi will love them, and look – they're marked down to one pound fifty. They're a bargain!'

Suzi may be Dad's girlfriend but, at twenty-three, she's not really that grown up, plus we share the same taste in

1

clothes. I was sure she would love the knickers – they were hardly sexy, frou-frou lingerie; they were more like cartoon knickers. *J'aime t'acheter des culottes* – as I expect they say in France. I bet all the girls wear polka-dot pants in Paris; when I live in Paris, I certainly will. *J'aime Paris.*

'What about Mum?' continued Poppy, my irritating elder sister. 'Have you thought about how she's going to feel when you give red pants to Dad's girlfriend?'

'I have thought, so I'm getting Mum the purple ones. Purple's more her colour really.'

'Lily, you're too ridiculous and stupid, I give up. I'm going to look for Nick's present.'

'Why don't you just buy it cheap in the Boxing Day sale since you're not seeing the boyfriend on Christmas Day?'

This seemed like one of my most sensible suggestions and I was even slightly shocked that I was being so kind as to share my obvious wisdom with my dumb sister.

Poppy glared back venomously – clearly it wasn't obvious to her. 'Actually, Nick's coming to us for Christmas dinner. He's seeing his parents in the morning and coming to see me after on his bike. Oh sorry, didn't Mum tell you?' She grinned at me like a caged beast.

'Yuck! You and Nick, Dad and Suzi – all that PDA,' (Public Displays of Affection). 'Yuck! Well, at least Mum, Bay and I can be normal together.'

'You'll have to be, since poor little you was dumped by your boyfriend.'

'Curl up and die, you female dog. He didn't dump me, you bucket of tiger-poo!'

'Whatever! I hope you're getting Nick a present.'

'Yes, you! It'll be the ugliest thing I can think of to give a gibbon,' I said and strode off.

The Annual Argy-Bargy

Every year my sister Poppy and I get together for our Annual Away Day Christmas Argy-Bargy, otherwise known as present shopping for Mum and Dad. This year promised to be especially exciting I thought, because there were going to be just two new people to get presents for – Suzi and Bay. But now it turned out smelly Nick was going to be there as well! Bay, our baby brother, didn't count the year before – he was so small that for a present I just gave him some boxes inside each other with lots of ribbon and wrapping paper. He thought they were great. No, really – hours of fun. But now he's three he's learned to become a demanding consumer. Mostly he wants swords and armour. I told Mum just to let him play with the kitchen knife and pan lids as he wouldn't know the difference, but she gave me one of her special looks, and shook her head. A lot of grown-ups do that around me and I still don't know what it means, though I think it might be disapproval. Maybe Bay could have a battle with Nick and mortally wound him gladiator-style.

Nick is my sister's worse-than-ugly eighteen-year-old new boyfriend. He used to be fat and roll around Battersea Park like a pot-bellied pig from the zoo, but then he got chicken pox and now he's all lanky and in a band for bad skin and grotty music. For some reason, Poppy thinks this makes him Mr Gorgeous. I think this means Poppy needs her eyes and ears testing.

Poppy and I don't shop well together, but it's become tradition to have our annual scream on Christmas Eve in Oxford Street; Christmas wouldn't be the same without it. Or maybe, it's because we can never think of what to buy our parents and, if pushed, we can put our money together and buy them each a box of posh chocolate truffles from the two of us. I don't see why we can't make truffles, though – I mean how hard can they be? Melt chocolate, add cream, roll in cocoa.

In the old days it was all so different – we were young and carefree and could get away with making a dish out of mud at school and painting it. Mum would usually think it was an ashtray and be really pleased, and for Dad you could do a drawing and he'd put it up in his office, as if it were a masterpiece. Everything changes as you get older, and not always for the best. Suddenly you're expected to compete in the expensive world of buying luxury goods, and on pocket money it's not fair – I can hardly afford the wrapping paper. I bet Bay wouldn't notice if I bought his present second-hand from an Oxfam shop. At least I can just make a card for Gran and that keeps her happy. She always goes away to New Zealand to see her friends for Christmas now, and I know why. The last time she was with us, Granny whispered to me, 'Sorry Lily, love, but I shan't be doing this again. It's too depressing.'

I knew just what she meant, as I watched Mum tear off a turkey leg and throw it at Dad's head. He ducked and it hit the Christmas tree, which crashed over into the presents. Dad stormed out of the house, slamming the door. Oh, and then all the lights fused. Dad came back later that night to get some things but, with the blackout, he couldn't find anything. It only took a couple of months for him to pack his cases and leave for good. That was three and half years ago when Mum was pregnant with Bay.

How To Make a Fun Christmas

Making Christmas fun is left up to Poppy, me and Bay. Let me revise that: me and Bay (Poppy has no sense of humour). But then again, Bay has a habit of breaking everything, so actually it's just up to me.

And I was just not getting that little thrill of *joie de vivre*, as they say in France. Ah, Christmas in Paris – now that would be civilised, and as soon as I'm old enough I'm skedaddling over there to live and work in the Shakespeare & Co. bookshop away from that hell they call Oxford Street, London, England.

I thought England was supposed to be a civilised country. Huh! I was suffocating. I was being trampled on and elbowed about amongst the millions of pre-Christmas shoppers flashing credit cards and jumping overboard; it was like a hysterical scene from *Titanic*.

Of course I was excited by Christmas, but all the mass consumerism seemed a little sick when people in Africa still don't have clean water to drink. I'm not saying I wanted to be given a goat instead of all my pressies, but if I were a grown-up I would, because, after all, it's not like Dad needs any more socks. I thought I might just write him a poem instead. I was thinking of all the words that rhyme with Dad – sad, lad, bad, fad – when Poppy pompously suggested, 'I think we should pool our money and get Dad this scarf.'

She is officially the bossiest sister in the world. She thinks just because she's three years older than me most of the year, she knows better. Older, she thinks, means wiser. But, as I have told her, being older just means that her brain is deteriorating faster.

Poppy continued to hold up the scarf amidst the massive crowd heaving through the shop. I wonder if this is what hell is like? Me and Poppy on Oxford Street at Christmas time, for ever.

'But that's so boring, Poppy,' I told her. 'Why don't we buy him a goat in Africa? Besides, didn't we give him a scarf last year?'

'Well, he liked it last year.'

'So he'll like it again this year? Are you *complètement toquée*?'

'He's probably lost it by now – you know how people always lose scarves. Scarves and umbrellas.'

'So are you suggesting we buy him a matching *parapluie*?'

'No, an umbrella. Gloves are the other thing.'

'Poppy, this conversation is making no sense to me at all.'

'Well, since when have Hennes sold goats?'

'You get them from Oxfam.'

'What if Bay gets too attached to it? We couldn't just put it on a plane to Africa after it had got to know the family.'

'Please, Poppy, tell me you're joking.'

I thought she had to be, but I couldn't be entirely sure that she didn't know the goats were already in Africa then given to families there in your name.

'Lily, Christmas isn't all about being funny. Come on – let's queue for a million years and pay for these. It's about the baby Jesus, turkey and Christmas pudding. Oh and being together as a family.'

'So why's SickNick coming if it's about family as you claim, huh?'

'Shut up, you're just jealous because you couldn't keep your boyfriend.'

That was a particularly underhanded dig to pull out again. I did have a boyfriend called Blake, and he is lovely, but – and it was a big but – he lives in Norfolk and I live in London, and though they're not a million miles away from each other it's hardly next door, and it's not like for my fourteenth birthday I got a chauffeur-driven Ferrari to zip up and down the motorway in – my father's mean like that. So the end result was I never got to see the beautiful Blake, and not seeing a boyfriend means you have a pen-friend. Nice when you're eight, less useful at fourteen. I mean, who am I meant to practise kissing with – and what's the point in going out, since you never get to, well, go out together? So Blake and I have amicably split up, but we have agreed that IF I ever move to Norfolk, or IF he ever moves to London, we will date. All of which means that neither of us was dumped, but we're both free to go out with other local people for the time being. Result. It does also mean that I don't have a boyfriend, so

8

technically Poppy is right. But being single and fancy-free is not all bad – it's one less person to buy a present for. Plus, if the truth be told, I didn't think Blake would really fit into my plans of living in Paris and being a poet on the Left Bank. He isn't really that sort of person – he doesn't understand Flaubert. Plus I suspect he might get jealous when I become a famous movie star in Hollywood. And there is nothing worse than someone who's jealous of your achievements – I just have to look at Poppy to realise that. As Granny 1 says, 'He who travels alone travels furthest.' Sometimes it's better to travel alone.

I started to imagine just how far I could get without Poppy; without any of my family. And then I remembered: I *was* going away without them. Within days I was off to Tangier with Maya, who is my best American buddy, as they say Stateside, who lives in London. I met her at a summer camp for the maladjusted, along with Blake, and we all got on instantly.

Maya is lucky enough not to have siblings, so together we were to have an adventure of a lifetime in the strange and mysterious land of Morocco. It was very exciting and made being in the bear pit with my family over Christmas almost bearable.

'Well Poppy, at least I don't stink like a skunk, and I get to lie by a pool amongst the exotica of Marocca.'

'It's Morocco, not Marocca, and it's not nice to boast,

Lily. There might be people in this queue who won't be going anywhere for Christmas, like me, and you're showing off about going to Morocco. Sometimes I don't think you've got a sensitive bone in your body.'

Sometimes Poppy just leaves me speechless. What happens when you combine shopping and Poppy? You get a basket-case called Shoppy! (Wonder if I can get a job writing the jokes in Christmas crackers?)

'What about rehab for Christmas, Poppy? That would be something you could go away and do with Nick.'

Poppy refused to sit with me on the bus home but only because I pretended to be a chimpanzee.

Sandwiching It All In

Slamming the front door, I shouted, 'Mum! I'm home. Can you make me a sandwich?'

Dumping my bag in the hall, I ran upstairs, still shouting, because that's the only way to get anyone to listen to you in this house. 'I've got to meet Bea. I'm so gonna be late if I go to the loo as well as make a sandwich.'

I heard Mum yell something.

'What? I can't hear you.'

'Don't worry, a cheese and pickle roll is already waiting on the table, Your Majesty' I heard her say audibly the third time, as I came out of the loo.

'But Mum, you know I hate pickle,' I said, jumping down the last bit of the staircase with a satisfying thump.

'Don't keep doing that, Lily, love. You don't like it because you don't eat it enough. If you ate it more, you'd like it. And this is special – it's posh Prince Charles pickle.' This sums up Mum's outlook.

'Just because it's posh doesn't mean it's better. I wouldn't like it even if it was made by the Queen. Can't I have the smoked salmon that I saw in the fridge?' I put a slight whine in the last syllable as it usually helps to get what I want.

'No. That's for Christmas Day. I've already told you – it's expensive and we're saving it for the guests.'

'But *I'm* one of the guests.' I tried to reason with her but it was clearly beyond her. 'Can't I have it now and then I won't have any tomorrow?'

My winning whining still wasn't working. 'No!' she said in a sharp un-Mum way. What had got into her? Something was clearly up!

'So, how come you're letting Poppy's baboon-bum Nick come here for dinner, and I don't get to invite anyone?' I said, giving in and stuffing the roll in my mouth.

'You never asked,' Mum said, as she got all the present-wrapping stuff on to the table. 'Now hurry up out, I've only got one Bay-free hour to do everything whilst he's over at his friend's.'

I was betting she wanted me out of the house to wrap up my billions of pressies. Nice Mum. 'But if I had asked a mate, you would've let me, right?' She nodded distractedly. I put my arm about her, and leaned my head on her shoulder. 'Ah, don't you worry, little Mama, I still love you. At least we'll be the gooseberries together: me, you and Bay. Three little gooseberries sitting in a row . . .' I sang to the tune of 'Ten Green Bottles'. 'And no one's allowed to do any disgusting PDA because I'll throw up,' I told her, stuffing another good chunk of roll in my mouth. 'This is yummy, even with the pickly stuff. You are the best mum in the world.'

Mum turned away, suspiciously quiet, and started to do the drying up. Now there's one thing I know about Mum – she never does the drying up, firmly believing that, if left alone, it dries itself.

'Hey, what's up, Mum? Why are you doing that?'

'Well, I want everything to be nice for tomorrow.'

'But you never usually care. Is this to do with Suzi coming?'

'A bit.'

'Oh, she wouldn't notice, she's not like that.' I was about to go on about how much she'd like her, if she gave her a chance, but I sensed that was enough talk on the subject of Dad's girlfriend. 'You can't be doing it for Nick, and certainly not for Dad.' Then a thought struck

12

my brain like lightning. 'There's nobody else coming, is there, Mum?'

There was a shudder of silence, so loud it seemed to walk in with arms, legs and a mouth to fill the kitchen. She wouldn't look at me.

'Mum?' And when she didn't answer right then, I knew. Oh my God, it was going to be the worst Christmas ever. It was Official. It was as bad as being attached to a cart and dragged along to the Tower of London in Ye Olden Days!

'I'm sorry, Lily, it's just . . .'

But I didn't wait around for the rest of her snivelling explanation. I grabbed my bag and ran out of the house as fast as my small, lumpy legs could go. The only place to be was my best friend Bea's house.

Thank You for Best Friends

'I know Mr Taylor's horrible, and he teaches citizenship so badly, but honestly, he's not the worst teacher to have in your house on Christmas Day. Imagine if you had the headmaster instead?'

I looked at my friend uncomprehendingly. 'And would you like to invite him over? No. There's no teacher I'd ever invite into my house. They're a breed from another world – they're like Mr McGregor to Peter Rabbit, like the evil witch from *The Wizard of Oz* –'

'I thought you said Mr Jordan who teaches A-level politics was "Well hot"?' she politely interrupted.

'He is. But I still wouldn't invite him home to meet my dad. You just can't understand how I feel. Imagine if it was your mother that was snogging and stuff with Mr Taylor? He probably even puts his tongue in her mouth!'

'Vomitorium. Sorry Lily, but when you put it like that . . .' Bea empathised.

'Exactly. Can I come over to your house for Christmas? Nobody wants me at home.'

'That's not true. Hey, why don't I try and come over to yours later on in the day and then we can play jokes on Mr Taylor – tie his laces together and put salt in his coffee.'

Bea was my best and oldest friend for a reason – she had a way of putting things that sounded very appealing. Friendship comes in all sorts of shapes and sizes, but the old ones are the best. Still, I felt a little unsettled. Beneath it all I felt Bea was trying to hide something from me. What was going on? I reckoned it had to be a boy who was making her go all funny – it had been going on for weeks now.

'You don't want me to come to yours, do you? Are you having your mystery boyfriend over?'

'No! I do want you over, Lily, but honestly, it's going to be so, so, so boring with Granddad going on about our manners and Gran fussing over the food and losing her teeth every ten minutes. And, and, we're seeing each other tonight, and on Boxing Day, and the day after, and the one after that . . .'

Suddenly it was me who felt guilty because I had neglected to tell her that I was going on holiday with Maya (who she doesn't get on with) the day after Boxing Day. I would be unavailable for buzzing about and generally loafing around with her. But at least Bea had someone to spend the hols with, even if she wouldn't tell me who it was. I suspected it was Martin, the little bug down our street. Ah, she was probably too embarrassed to tell me because he's so short.

I didn't want to tell her then and start a row, what with the way she felt about Maya. I had enough to deal with. At least I could escape to another world after the massive delights that awaited me on Christmas Day. Walking back home, I reminded myself that I was lucky, seriously. I would try to be less miserable, if only because it has a way of making you feel worse. But remembering how to smile all the time isn't always easy either. Wonder if you can have a smile tattoo put on your face and if you could, would it make you feel any better? So many questions . . .

Watch the Brussels Sprout

'Have you finished those, Lily? How many times do I have

to tell you, Poppy! Can you just keep Bay out of the kitchen, please? It's dangerous.'

Mum was at her most relaxed. I swear I could see steam escaping out of her ears like an old train. She always likes to prepare as much of Christmas dinner as possible the night before.

The oven was also puffing out steam from roasting the chestnuts. The stuffing was being stuffed, the turkey was groaning . . . no, that was Mum trying to turn the turkey over, and the sprouts were making that horrible Brussely smell without even being cooked.

I was topping and tailing the green beans as I was officially in charge of vegetables (I was used to it with my family). I was also being quite handy around the mince pies – I'd made all the pastry after getting back home.

I had decided to be nice to Mum because Dad was coming with Suzi, and that must be terrible for her – so terrible that she had to invite Mr Taylor, and she must be desperate if Mr Taylor was the only person she could get to go out with her. It wasn't actually Mum's fault that he was so awful – obviously it must be his parents'.

Suddenly I was overflowing with Christmassy goodwill, and I was soon to be swamped with lovely pressies. The day after that I had to pack, and then – yippee! I was going away on a plane to the exotic. I would just have to grit my teeth and hide from Torturous

Taylor. I could always give him Bay to play with, but then that might be too cruel even for a little monster like Bay.

'Don't forget, the dining-room table has to be completely cleared!' Mum screamed to Poppy across the BBC Radio 4 presenter. Mum always has the radio on – I'm sure she doesn't even listen half the time.

'I know, Mum.' I jumped up. 'Why don't we have some nice Christmassy music on that we can sing along to? I can find something now that I've finished doing the beans, and the mince-pie pastry is all ready and one batch can go in the oven.'

'Oh darling Lily, you are good.' I smiled angelically back. I was, wasn't I? 'Thank you, darling, I don't know what I'd do without you. I'm going to tell your father what a help you've been and make sure he gives you a nice lump of spending money for Morocco. You deserve it. Look at those mince pies, they look good enough to eat. Can Bea and her mum have some when they come over later?'

'Yes. Isn't that the idea with mince pies – that you eat them?' Poor Mum.

'What, oh, yes. And Lil, I really am so sorry I didn't tell you about Mr Taylor coming, but it's just his parents both live in Spain.'

I nodded my head understandingly. Quite frankly, I didn't blame them. Imagine having a child like that! They probably ran away to escape him.

'And Christmas is a time for sharing. We have this lovely family, and not everyone is as lucky as us.'

CRASH! BANG! 'Oh Bay, how could you be so stupid? You useless snotpoo!' screamed Poppy hysterically.

Bay started crying 'Mama! Mama!' and ran into the kitchen to be comforted.

'Oh, Poppy! Now what did you do to poor Bay?' demanded Mum.

'What d'ya mean? He ruined my box of make-up, and, as usual, it's "Poor Bay"! This family is twisted, no wonder nobody appreciates me. And what are you looking at, koala-brain?' Poppy scowled at me like a demented evil troll.

I smiled back and thought, Mum was so right; not everyone is as lucky as us, to have such a lovely, and loving, family at Christmas time.

CHAPTER TWO

Peace on Earth

25th December – Keeping Occupied

'Mum? Mum, are you awake yet? Can I open my presents, Mum?'

As grown up and mature as I most definitely am, as soon as Christmas Day arrives, I always revert back to being about five years old. I think I'll always be like that. I can't help but wake up, giddy with excitement, at six in the morning to the warm feeling of a stocking full of tangerines, plums and chocolates, a paperback book usually, a magazine or comic, some nail polish or fake tattoo transfers, and some nuts I can never crack – all things Father Christmas knows make me happy while I'm lazing around in bed on that special day.

Bay decided otherwise. He crept into my room at dawn,

stealing my magical moments with the lightness of a heffalump, wellies on his feet and a Viking helmet on his head. First he stuck his finger in my eye to see if I was properly awake (if I wasn't before, I certainly was then) and then he stuck one up my nose, obviously to test if I was still breathing. If he ever puts one in my mouth, he'll be left with nine fingers and I swear I won't be responsible. Then we played with his toys until it was an almost acceptable hour to bother Mum.

'Not yet, darlings,' groaned Mum. 'Why don't you wait? It's still the middle of the night.' She pulled a pillow over her head, imitating an ostrich with its head in the sand. Useless!

'Mum, we can still see you and it's morning. Bay and I have been awake for hours.' We had too – for two hours.

'Have you looked in your stocking? What on earth is the time? Bay, darling, please don't sit on Mummy's head.'

'It's late – past eight.' Technically true, if only by one minute.

Suddenly Mum was struggling quickly out of bed, desperately trying to find her dressing gown and slippers, reminding me of a beetle on its back, struggling to right itself.

'I've got to get that turkey on, the bread sauce made, and the brandy butter for the Christmas pudding. Help! Does anyone really like brandy butter?'

'I like bandybutta, I like bandybutta . . .' Bay kept repeating over and over, with no notion of what it meant. *Les petits enfants sont très étranges*, or maybe it's just Bay.

'Hello, Mum? Mum, can't you remember anything? Whilst Bea and I cooked mince pies last night, you were busy drinking the brandy with Angela. We made double lots of the butter for them, too. Remember?' I wiggled my fingers like an expert hypnotist in front of her eyes. 'It's all coming back to you. Angela and you and the brandy. When I clap my hands you will remember everything.' I clapped my hands. 'Even, that it's Christmas Day.'

'Sorry, Lily. Come here you two.' She grabbed me and Bay to give us each a kiss and a wraparound hug, as she got up. 'Happy Christmas, my little Lily love.'

She opened the curtains and glorious blue sky, brightened by a now visible sun, shone through the window. 'What a lovely day for Christmas. C'mon, downstairs, you monsters, just wait for me to put some clothes on,' she said, chasing us round with a fat growl that made Bay screech with laughter.

Mum was suddenly alive and smiling. Which proves you should never be sympathetic to adults when they groan – they're just trying to get attention and are much better off if they're up and about and making comments about the weather, like they always do!

Bay revved up his special screech engine as he jumped

up and down on the bed, and then came the inevitable tears and sobs as he jumped up and fell off the side, hitting the wooden floor with a healthy clunk. Tears before we'd even had breakfast.

Bay Must Pay

There was loads of clearing up to do, so I tried to keep Bay occupied whilst Mum got on with it. Well, I couldn't do everything! Just as I was getting him some juice, the little monster grabbed my *pain au chocolat* and stuffed it into his mouth, laughing!

'Grrr, just you wait, Bay. You've eaten my breakfast once too often, and there's only one thing for me to do. I'm going to have to eat you up.' I grabbed him and gave him a massive tickle, and he laughed so much all his face crunched and his eyes welled up with tears, and I couldn't help laughing as well.

'Goddamnyou, shurrup! What's all this noise? I can't get any sleep!' shouted a very grumpy voice from upstairs.

'I wonder which beautiful princess's voice that can be? Why, Poppy? A very merry Christmas to you too! Are you playing the part of Scrooge this year?'

Poppy staggered, floppy-pyjama-clad and with hair like a scarecrow's, into the room and then collapsed on the sofa with all the animation of a zombie.

It was then that I realised, what with all the cooking and laughter, that I hadn't wrapped her presents last night. She stuck her tongue out at me. 'Smellpot, make me a cup of coffeeee, pleeeze.'

'Mum's just making some. I'll get you one as long as you make sure Bay doesn't disturb Mum. She's involved in very important, top secret cooking and washing up duties. I've got to go upstairs and wrap her pressie,' I whispered.

'Thought you did that last night?'

'No, just made the card,' I white-lied.

'OK, go on then. Call me if you need help bringing my enormous present down. I notice there's nothing for me under the tree.'

'No, that's fine – I think I can manage a radish. That was what you wanted, wasn't it?'

'Ha, ha, smelly.'

I ran upstairs and grabbed the necessaries. Her presents might not have cost me anything – they were all samples from a department store – but I had got some major stuff for Poppy. However much we might pretend to loathe each other, she is my sister after all. There was a mini mascara, lip-gloss, spot cover-up and an eye pencil, and some perfumes – *Joe and Paul* and *Poison* – perfect for carrying around in a make-up bag. I was sure Mum wouldn't recognise it as the red pencil case she'd bought me and I hadn't used. All I had to do was write *EMERGENCY* on it using Mum's white nail polish – *voilà! Très chic*, if I do say so myself. I put it in tissue paper and tied it with a great bow, then I carried it with all the other presents downstairs to put beneath the tree.

I was feeling extremely proud of my presents this year: for Bay, the cutest little cowboy outfit including gun, holster and hat; Mum's purple satin pants with the polka-dot green bow; Dad's glove (Poppy was giving him the other one) and Suzi's red pants. *Quel choix excellent!* I congratulated myself. It's not what they cost, it's the imagination and thought that counts. I could practically qualify as a personal shopper if I wasn't going to live in Paris, be a poet and a Hollywood film star. People don't always realise how hard it is to be so, so, so very talented!

Dear Diary,
It is nearly the end of you – farewell, old friend, you who have some of the most important parts of my soul smudged across your pages. Nothing I write will ever be as poetic, hilarious or heart-squashing as this year's traumas. You, dear diary, who have been witness to my darkest nights and loneliest days, the truth of my love for Hot Billy next door, my hatred for cheesehead sket Amanda, my love for beautiful Blake . . . (It seems that I can only be in love with boys beginning with B – curious. I'm sure I absolutely could

not fall in love with anyone called Barry, Bartholomew or Bert.) Only you know how I've felt about the cruelty of my evil parents. (Though of course Mum is great today because it's Christmas.) As for piggy Poppy . . .

I want to write about how miserable Christmas Day with Mr Taylor is, but he hasn't arrived yet, so that will have to wait.

I've opened my pressies from Mum – we were allowed to open two. The first is an amazing green dress and the second is a beautiful new diary, but I can't exactly play with it till next year, can I? Meanwhile, don't be jealous, dear diary . . .

I could be slowly dissolving on the sofa with starvation, and who would notice? Bay's collapsed on the floor, asleep in front of Robin Hood. *Poppy's trying to make herself beautiful for Nick's arrival, so that'll take weeks, and Mum is in the kitchen, after just having fancied herself up with too much perfume, lipstick and blusher. Can it be for Mr Taylor's sake?!!*

<u>A Christmas Poem</u>
Oh, when will the circus begin?
The presents and feasts, my sister's a beast,
Can I really be bothered to join in?

I wonder when I will be Poet Laureate?

Mr Burns's Bottom

'When's dinner? I'm starving, Mum.' I wandered into the kitchen to see Mum still dashing around.

'It'll be ready when the guests arrive. Have a smoked salmon and cream cheese bagel. Besides, the turkey isn't cooked yet. It still needs an hour and then we have to let it sit before Dad can carve it. So dinner will be in an hour and half, as long as everyone's on time.'

'Can you bring the bagel over here, Mum?'

'No, I'm cooking. Do it yourself.'

'Why are you so cruel?'

'Come and help me with the parsnips.'

'Hardly answers the question, plus I don't like parsnips and they don't like me.'

'Well, lay the table then. Don't forget the glasses and the napkins.'

'Don't worry, I've got them.'

'Not *The Simpsons* ones, Lily. I don't think Pat would appreciate wiping his mouth on Mr Burns's bottom.'

'Pat? *Quoi? Qui est Pat?* We're not having another surprise guest are we?' Of course I knew the answer, I just wanted to hear her say it.

'Pat. Patrick Taylor. Mr Taylor.' Mum's voice was all squeaky whilst her face blushed pinker than her make-up.

'But Pat's a girl's name, Mum. How could you? Do you

call him Patsy for short?' I said, laughing hysterically. It was very funny.

'Oh, stop being so silly, Lily, and come and help me turn this bird over.'

Ding Dong Merrily on High
I had just finished basting (that's a highly technical chef term for pouring the grease in the tin over the dry bits) the roast potatoes and parsnips, when *ding dong*.

'That's them, Mum, I'll get the door,' I shouted out.

'Shouldn't you get dressed first, Lily? I'll answer the door. I'm sure it's Pat.' She appeared hideously wreathed in smiles. (I think the term 'glowing' could've been applied. They always glow in Victorian novels, when men arrive.)

I'd completely forgotten I hadn't got dressed. Luckily I stopped just in time. Yikes. Imagine if Mr Taylor (I cannot think of him as Pat) saw me in my PJs? I ran faster than the wind, sweeping my diary and new dress up into my arms.

Nightmare in Battersea
What's worse than Mr Taylor seeing me in PJs? Worse than seeing him in his PJs? Mr Taylor reading my diary. No. Mr Taylor reading my diary out in assembly . . . naked! Must stop scaring myself with daytime

nightmares. It was bad enough hearing the pluck and squish of kisses, the girlish giggles, and Mum's voice go up an octave. Mum's forty-three, Mr Taylor's twenty-eight. There should be a rule against it. I mean Dad's worse – he's forty-seven and Suzi's twenty-three, but that's just plain pervy. When I get married, IF I ever choose to get married, I'm going to be with someone the same age as me, otherwise how would they know about all the music and television programmes that you watched as a kid? You'd have nothing in common.

Which Led Me to Think . . .

I wonder what's happened to Billy, our hot next-door neighbour, who's a couple of years older than me. At least ham-faced Amanda isn't slouching around him any longer. I wonder if he could be my Christmas project? I wonder if he'd like a homemade mince pie? It would be a good excuse to knock on his door.

After all that thinking I had to get dressed double-quick. My lip-gloss and mascara were almost running out – I shouldn't have been so generous to Poppy. The shiny river-green dress Mum had got me was fantastic – I suspected Poppy might have helped choose it – and it fitted brilliantly and matched my eyes. Since it's Fifties'-style, I put my hair up in a ponytail and wore my largest hoop earrings, ballet pump shoes and a short cardigan with a large belt. Then I was ready to meet the world! I was just wondering how I was going to make Mum realise that I was on my way down, so that I wouldn't have the embarrassment of catching her and Mr Taylor snogging – I have seen Mum snog boyfriends in the past and it is not a pretty sight – when the doorbell rang again.

'Poppy,' I screamed. 'It's Dad. Dad and Suzi are here.'

That should stop Mum and Mr Taylor, I thought, as I tore towards the door, without even having said hello to 'Pat'.

Present Behaviour

'Happy Christmas, Dad, Suzi,' I said, opening the door and getting lots of kisses. 'God, it's so nice to see you! Come in. Shall I take your coats for you? Mum! It's Dad and he's got a bag full of champagne and Guinness – your favourite. I'll just get glasses.'

'Well, thank you. What a hostess,' said Dad, impressed, as Mum appeared behind me. 'Merry Christmas, Jenny. Anything we can do to help? Where's Bay?'

'Out cold on the floor. Try not to step on him. Just sit down and relax,' she told him.

'Hi Dad,' Poppy screamed, running down the stairs wearing, if I was not mistaken, the sailor dress I'd bought for Morocco. 'Have you got me loads of pressies?'

'Wait and see, you wicked daughter. Say hello to Suzi.'

'Hello. Mum, anything you want me to carry in?'

'What are you doing wearing my dress, Poppy?' I hissed at her, as we went into the sitting room.

'It looks good on me, doesn't it? I was bored with all my clothes – you don't mind, do you?'

'Yes, I do! Take it off. Now.'

'Make me.' She smiled that evil Poppy smile.

'Mum! She's wearing my holiday dress. She'll ruin it!'

'No, I'm not, because this is actually my dress. It just looks the same as yours. Go and check your wardrobe. Ha ha, got ya!'

'Stop arguing, girls,' Mum intervened. 'Who's getting the champagne and glasses, and taking the smoked salmon plate thing?' she called out from the kitchen.

I was fuming. Poppy did anything just to wind me up. Why had she bought the same dress as me? People might think we were twins! What a revolting thought.

'Poppy, can you just take the salmon in?' I asked, taking charge because Mum was simpering and giggling again with Mr Taylor by the fridge, so much so she was practically incapable of conversation. Who'd imagine that a teacher could possibly have that effect? What had they been up to? Actually, I didn't want to know!

'Of course, Lilypad.' Poppy was still laughing at me as we went into the kitchen.

'This is Pat Taylor,' I said, introducing them. 'This is Poppy, my evil sister.'

'Hi.' He smiled nervously and, for the first time ever, I felt a minuscule *petit peu* sorry for him. It wasn't his fault he was my teacher. Or maybe it was. He could have chosen to do something else in this world.

'Come and meet my dad and Suzi,' I said, being really nice.

'It's all right, love. Let's all get out of the kitchen together. Not long and the food will be ready.' Mum ushered us all into the sitting room.

'Hi, Suzi, what a lovely dress! This is my friend Pat, Pat Taylor. Pat this is Peter, Suzi, Poppy, and Bay is the one flat-out on the cushion beneath the tree. And of course you know Lily.'

Dad said how lovely the tree was and it really was – massive and green and smelling of pine. Suzi said how beautiful the house was, especially the wood-burning stove and chimney that Mum had only just put in, which made Dad grimace, because he hadn't wanted to pay for it. She also said how lovely my dress was and that she could only drink non-alcoholic organic drinks. I suggested water. She seemed strangely compliant for Suzi, almost dozy. Pat said how good Mum's paintings were and Dad poured the champagne and Guinness together. It is the traditional grown-up Lovitt Christmas drink. It's called a Black Velvet and doesn't taste too disgusting for one sip. Then Dad raised a toast for a lovely day, dinner and another great year ahead.

Regarde, Très Weird

I slipped upstairs and looked in my wardrobe. My dress was still there, but my new patent ballet pumps were gone. I knew she'd taken something. I would get my own back. There were definite pluses and minuses to being the same size as your big sister – borrowing is never a one-way street. I wondered what to borrow for Morocco.

Bay woke up and was quite sweet and entertained everyone as Poppy and I helped Mum get the dinner out and on to the table. For once everyone seemed Happy with a capital H – even nice, because they were too busy eating to talk, apart from pleasantries about the food and cooking, which must have been good – Suzi had double helpings! Poppy was the exception, as always. She was in a foul mood because Nick hadn't turned up and wasn't answering his mobile.

'Why don't you just call him at home? I'm sure his parents won't mind,' Dad said.

'You don't understand, Dad. None of you understand anything, just butt out,' Poppy snapped. She was right about that, we didn't understand. She trembled on the edge of crying until her eyes couldn't cope with any more water and overflowed with the sort of free flow of tears you see only in movies.

'So Pat, how do you fill your days on this lovely planet of ours?' said Dad, weirdly, as if Mr Taylor was a visitor from outer space.

'Why don't you just ask him what he does for a living? That's what you want to know, isn't it?' I said, because I didn't want Dad to sound like a loony, for Mum's sake, even if he was on his fifth glass.

'Yes, thank you, Lily, exactly. So?' asked Dad.

'Mr Taylor is Lily's citizenship teacher at school,' Poppy said. 'What, Mum? It's true.' Poppy had mysteriously spoken through her veil of tears.

Poor Mum was suddenly trying to explain that they hadn't met at a Parent-Teacher evening and that Pat's main job was teaching geography. Dad just gave Mum all these weird looks and stuck his chest out like some stag in the forest wanting to lock antlers. I made a funny face at Suzi, which made her laugh, which made Mum angry, and I didn't think I'd ever hear myself say it, but *merci mon Dieu!* Nick finally arrived as we were finishing the main course, hiccupping and stumbling and helped to divert everyone's attention. Poppy led him into the kitchen for some water. 'Sorry, babe,' he kept on saying. 'But I do love you, babe.'

All pretty hilarious – I only wished I'd had Bea or Maya

33

there to share it with me. Never mind, it would keep. Dad meanwhile fumed not only because of Pat, but Nick too, slouching all over Poppy shouting, 'Poppy is the most beautiful girl in the world. She's like the sun on a cloudy day. From now on, every song I write is going to be called "Poppy", 'cos I love yer. What rhymes with Poppy?'

Ploppy, shoppy, sloppy, I thought to myself.

'Who is this Nick boy? How old is he?' Dad mouthed to Mum, who tried to calm him.

'It's all right, Peter, he's from a nice family and he's eighteen. He's in quite a successful band you know.'

I don't think she could have said anything worse to Dad. She must have forgotten that Dad always wanted to be in a band and because he wasn't, he hates all of them now and only listens to Wagner and Mahler.

'Why on earth are you allowing her to go out with a drug-addicted, drink-addled waste of space, Jenny? Are you completely stupid?'

'Actually, Peter, he's a pretty decent boy with good A-level results – he only left school in the summer,' said Pat. Mum smiled gooey appreciation at him. Dad noticed and fumed, his nostrils flaring so that all his nose hair seemed to stick out at once.

'And you'd know that, because . . .? Were you in the same class as him at school?'

'Yes, if you're asking if I taught him,' answered Mr

Taylor crisply. He really did look too young to be arguing with Dad.

'What do they say about teachers? "People who can, do. People who can't, teach?" Is that how it goes? What was it that you couldn't do, Pat, apart from my wife, eh?'

'Dad!' screamed Poppy and I, and Bay joined in for good measure, always willing to increase the sound levels.

'Peter!' screamed Suzi and Mum, both equally horrified, as if Dracula was coming towards them.

'I don't mind you insulting me, Peter, but I do mind you being rude in front of Jenny and the children.' Mr Taylor was sounding just like he did in the classroom. I wouldn't have been surprised if he'd said, 'Detention!' or 'Go to the headmaster's office NOW!' But he didn't. Instead he said, 'I've dealt with fifteen-year-old hooligan boys who were, quite frankly, better behaved than you. Now please apologise to your *ex*-wife.'

'Don't think you can come into my house, you little whippersnapper, and start telling me what to do.' Dad was standing and yelling now.

'Peter, it's not your house, it's mine, and how dare you point at Pat and bring his age into it. A long time ago you were young too,' Mum snapped. 'I wasn't going to be rude enough to mention it, Peter, but have you forgotten how old you are, and that Suzi is barely older than your own daughters?'

Poor Suzi turned puce-red and looked away. Poppy was busy snogging Nick behind the tree. Enough was enough. I had to get them all to realise that there were some priorities at Christmas, and that Bay was present.

'Mum! Dad! Can you just stop it! What's wrong with you? We haven't even had pudding yet and it's Christmas. Why does Christmas always end up like this, with you two rowing? Why can't you just make an effort for Bay?'

'Yes, me,' said Bay, clapping and enjoying the attention.

'Now apologise and clear the table so that we can have presents and pudding. I didn't go to the effort of making all that brandy butter for nothing.'

Guns and Knickers

Once I'd told them how to behave, Mum and Dad were quite good.

There were lots of pressies, which was nice. Bay charged around with his cowboy hat and gun in his hand, shooting everyone.

'I think Bay likes my present best,' I said, smugly.

'Lily, did you have to give him a gun?' asked Mum, as if I'd personally just added to crime on the streets.

'It's better than being prodded by his plastic sword all the time, and what's wrong with playing Cowboys and Indians?'

36

'It's not very politically correct – not many Native Americans survived,' said Mr Taylor helpfully.

'What lovely knickers!' exclaimed Suzi and Mum at the same time, before bursting out laughing, stopping Mr Taylor from lecturing us all about Pocahontas.

Suzi got me some new jeans and Mickey Mouse ears, which were really cool. Dad gave me a proper wallet with lots of lovely spending money inside. Mr Taylor even got a surprise present from me – a surprise because I didn't know I'd bought him a bottle of whisky. It was just as well though, because he gave me a book by a Moroccan writer called Mohammed Mrabet, who lived in Tangier. Luckily it was translated. He then tried to give me a geography lesson about Tangier and the Straits and the place where the Mediterranean meets the Atlantic, at which point I offered to fill the dishwasher rather than have to sit through any more.

Mum brought out the pudding, blue and orange flames licking at the small amount of brandy left over from the night before. We turned the lights out, held hands and made wishes for the year ahead. Everyone said my brandy butter was delicious, even if it had curdled a bit.

What Happened Next?

I'm not sure what happened next or in what order. We'd

finished eating the pudding, and I was just checking if there was any film worth watching on telly, when suddenly there was a fight between Dad and Pat over the whisky. The whisky was spilled, then someone knocked the candle over on to the tablecloth, and suddenly the smoke alarm was screeching and Mum was throwing jugs of water over everyone. Either before, during or after this, Nick was sick. Poppy cried and said Nick must have been allergic to something he ate.

Chaos reigned, the next-door neighbour came to see if she should call the fire brigade, nobody could turn the smoke alarm off, and the air was filled with a strange mixture of scents – burned tablecloth, whisky and vomit.

At that point I decided to gather up my presents, some biscuits and juice, borrow Mum's portable TV from her room, and barricade myself in my room. I decided that I wouldn't leave until it was time to go to the airport. For once they could tidy up their own mess. I had had quite enough of my family. Animals were more civilised than them.

I locked the door, put away my stuff and plugged in the TV. As I drew the curtains, I tried to forget the riot that was happening downstairs, and looked out on one of those peaceful scenes of Christmas night. It wasn't quite snowing but it was certainly sleeting. I heard a voice outside, but I could only see Billy, our lovely next-door neighbour, dancing in the road like a loony. If I opened the window and stuck my head out, he'd see me, but what would I say? I'd never been able to talk to Billy. I'd had too much of a crush on him for too long. Finally, he pulled someone out of his house and kissed her on the pavement. I could tell it wasn't Aardvark Amanda, his ex, but then I heard a voice say, 'No, not here.' Giggle. 'What if Lily saw us?'

'I don't care, I don't care,' Billy shouted, spinning her around. And then I saw it was Bea. Bea and Billy! No wonder she didn't want to tell me about the boy she was seeing – she knew how long I'd liked Billy.

For a minute I didn't know what to do, to feel, to think. I stood there frozen, staring after Bea and Billy, who were now skipping up the road – probably to her house. A rush of emotion flooded through me. I felt terribly, terribly sorry for myself. Everyone seemed to have someone, except me. How had Bea got together with Billy? What did Bea have that I didn't? Apart from the obvious – long legs, amazing figure, beautiful face . . . What did I have that she didn't? Pit pony legs, frizzy hair, a custard-soaked sponge-cake face that went pink in the sun . . . Oh, and a permanent F in maths.

Of course I was glad that Bea was happy. Bea hadn't had a proper boyfriend before, and much as it pained me, they did suit each other, both being so good-looking. But that didn't make it fair. Beautiful people should be spread evenly amongst the not-so-beautiful.

I put on my PJs and got into bed, my stomach full of food, my heart full of emptiness. In the background I could hear Bay crying, adults arguing and doors slamming. I did the only sensible thing I could and turned the volume of the TV up, snuggled down into my covers and tried to imagine how wonderful Tangier would be. I looked at the guidebook Dad gave me, whilst watching a really old movie. It was all about Christmas, and it was called *It's a Wonderful Life*! Sometimes God has a weird sense of humour.

CHAPTER THREE
The Aftermath of War

26th December – Five Portions

It was seven o'clock and Bay still hadn't woken me up, *quelle surprise!* Hooray! Never take anything for granted – celebrate each minor triumph in life, like sleeping past seven. I carefully trod over the piles of stuff crowding the staircase – shoes, coats and piles of presents: the usual Christmas clutter.

My belly was demanding that I got up. The problem with eating large meals is that it makes you ever so hungry the next morning, and food was all I could think about. I was starving, and I hoped the kitchen was full of food. In fact the kitchen was full of empty bottles and dirty plates and actually was more like a bomb site. The sitting room was worse – even the Christmas tree looked like it was trying to escape out of the French windows.

Now I am not a girl who minds a bit of mess (see my room) but this looked like the aftermath of war. Luckily, someone had cleared up Nick's sick – yuck! – but more had to be done. I tidied up a bit, but hunger got the better of me. I made the largest turkey sandwich in history, smothered with Mum's homemade tangy cranberry sauce (one of my five portions of fruit and vegetables), and a hot chocolate with marshmallows (not one of my five portions of f&v), before I settled down to the computer.

I had promised Granny 1 (Mum's mum in New Zealand) that I would keep her updated, since she had just bought herself a new Blackberry (she prides herself on being very modern). Not that she needed to know every grimy detail – just enough to know she was better off where she was. Plus I had to say thank you for a whole fifty Euro note, even if she doesn't realise that Morocco isn't part of Europe.

After that, I sent an email to Granny 2 in the south of France to say thank you for my present – twenty pounds' worth of book tokens to spend in the airport.

Every year those are my most important Christmas thank-yous. Once done, I wouldn't have to worry about anything whilst I was away. I could even try and forget about Dad's behaviour, and that terrible look on Suzi's face as Mum and Dad launched into each other. That was the last time I was going to think about that. I wasn't going to think about Billy and Bea either. I wish there was a forgetting potion I could drink. Why does anyone ever want to be an archaeologist and dig up the past?

Homicidal Washing Up

After I'd finished my granny email duty, I started to clear the sofa so I could watch TV. But when I sat down I got a shock – something definitely moved under me. Now I have heard about poltergeists and I was not prepared to have them in my house! Slowly I peeled back the big furry rug covering the sofa, which is usually on the floor, to see – aargh! If I hadn't known better I'd have thought it was *un animal!* Nick was staring up at me! We both screamed. He sat up terrified, and I sprang back. Upstairs, doors started opening; voices started moaning, groaning and shouting, 'Shurrup!'

Charming. An axe-murderer could have been attacking me and all my family would've said was, 'Shut up! Be quiet.'

'Where's Poppy? Who are you? You're not Poppy,' said Nick, looking like a complete trollhead.

'That's the nicest thing you've ever said to me,' I replied. 'I'm Lily, her sister, remember? Poppy's upstairs in her room.'

'Oh,' he said, standing up. 'Ouch – my head.'

'But I wouldn't go and see her.'

'Why not?'

'Because even she says she looks like the Wreck of the Hesperus in the morning before she's had a cup of coffee and brushed her hair.'

'What's the Wreck of the Hare's Berof?'

'A boat that crashed on to some rocks.'

'Oh, so what should I do, Lily?' Nick wasn't very smart but at least he knew it. Maybe he wasn't as bad as I'd always thought.

'Wait here. I'll make her a cup of coffee and wake her up. You can do some washing up if you're bored. At least somebody cleaned up your sick.'

'Oh my God, I was sick last night. Do you think your mum will forgive me? I must have been allergic to something I ate.'

'Yes – not what you drank. Still, if you do the washing up, she'd forgive homicide.'

I have never seen a boy put on washing-up gloves faster. It was great because Mum always expects Poppy and me to do the washing up on Boxing Day. Nick was OK.

Waking the Wreck

'Wakey, wakey!' I tapped on Poppy's door lightly. 'It's me – Lily.'

'Bug off, I'm asleep.'

'Wake up! Nick's downstairs and wanted to wake you up, but I thought you'd at least want to brush your hair!'

'What? Where's the mirror? Pass my brush.'

I let myself in. 'And here's your coffee.'

'Thanks, sis. Sorry about your shoes,' she said guiltily.

I looked for my new ballet pumps and saw them, splattered with a revolting tomato and carrot mix. 'Poppy!' I screamed. 'What is that stuff?'

'Keep your hair on. I'll get Nick to wash the sick off.'

Mr Taylor Speaks

I tipped Nick the wink to go upstairs to Poppy and, after I'd showered and dressed, I was going downstairs when I overheard voices coming from the kitchen. I wasn't really spying – I was more of an observer from the banisters.

'That's it! I've had as much of this screaming, hysterical family as I can take. It's bad enough at school, Jenny, but this is worse.'

'Worse than the staffroom? Or worse than the classroom?' Mum asked quizzically, raising one eyebrow whilst smiling and making a pot of tea. She seemed unusually calm. But what was Mr Taylor still doing in our house? Had he stayed over? Double yuck and vomit! But thankfully I noticed he wasn't wearing the same clothes as yesterday.

'Both. And the worst thing is, Jenny, you don't even seem to notice the chaos. Isn't it time you opened your eyes and really looked at your life?'

At which point I could see Bay, the monster cowboy, his hat having slipped over his eyes, charging right into Mr Taylor with his gun.

Mr Taylor screamed.

'Oh that's nice,' Mum was saying. 'You enjoy the hospitality of our family over Christmas and then you have the audacity to complain about the mess. Well, let me tell you, Pat, my *raison d'être* is not to be a housewife. I am a painter and a mother. Those things are the priorities in my life. Stuff the rest. And I think it's looking all rather tidy down here, thanks to the lovely Nick clearing up.'

At that point I thought it best to come downstairs if only to stop any potential row. I'd had enough of those for one Christmas.

'I'm starving, Mum, when are we eating? Oh, hi, Mr Taylor, so you're still here?'

'Pat just came back to pick up some things he'd left behind,' Mum said.

'And don't your children ever do anything around here? They're spoilt. When I was their age —'

'Actually, I did loads of clearing up, at eight this morning.' That shut him up.

46

'I'm sure.' Mum tousled my hair and I smiled smugly back at her.

'Well I'm going,' said Mr Taylor.

'Oh, must you, Pat? I was just going to make something to eat. Stay, sit down and relax – this is family life. Chill out!'

'I want to go poo, I want to go poo,' Bay shouted as he jumped around the room, at which point he dragged a potty from behind a curtain and sat on it, smiling.

'Oh, Bay, you're meant to take your trousers down first,' I said.

'I think I've lost my appetite, Jenny. I've got to go. We'll speak,' Mr Taylor said in the same way that Schwarzenegger said, 'I'll be back' – it was hard not to laugh. And at that, he turned on his heel and almost ran out, slamming the door behind him.

'Oh, no chance of a farewell kiss then?' Poppy called sarcastically, as she ran down the stairs, arms flung out.

'I'll give you a kiss, come 'ere,' laughed Nick, chasing after her into the kitchen. 'I thought he was going to give the lot of us detention.'

'Poor bloke, it's not his fault,' said Mum, pottering around the kitchen. 'He's not used to normal families – he's an only child and his parents live abroad. They probably do things differently over there.'

'Mum, they do things differently from our family

everywhere,' I pointed out.

'When's the food going to be ready?' Poppy asked. Nick and I want to eat and watch a movie. Don't we, Nick?'

'But we always play Monopoly on Boxing Day,' I said.

'And we always argue about it,' said Mum.

'We always do that anyway, whatever we're doing,' I pointed out.

'Maybe it's better not to. Poppy's right, maybe we can just veg a little and watch a movie,' Mum said, whilst picking up Bay and throwing him over her shoulder. 'You little stinker! Upstairs with you, clean-up time. Lily, love, why don't you see Bea? Remember, you're going off tomorrow.'

How could I forget? I wanted to see Bea, but how could I, with all that I knew, and that she didn't know that I knew. Why was life so complicated? Where was God when you needed answers?

'Why don't you ask her round for lunch? You could play Monopoly with her?'

'Can I borrow your phone and text her?'

'Have you still not topped up your phone? Honestly, do I have to do everything for you?'

'Yes, please.' I smiled cheesily at her. I picked up Mum's phone and plucked up the courage to text Bea.

R u Buzzy? Want to come over and play bored games?

She replied faster than was humanly poss.

Zut alors! Thought u'd never ask. Over in 30.

Bea Truthful Time

I'd finished packing and was reading when Bea came into my room, or at least that's what it looked like I was doing. Actually I was day-dreaming. Books are like magic carpets sometimes, whisking you away and leading you off to lovely places.

'Happy Christmas! What you reading, Lilo?' She walked in jauntily, picked up the book and jumped on the bed beside me. '*Tales of Morocco*? Oooo!'

'Thought I'd better get in the mood.'

'For what?'

'I don't know why I haven't told you. I mean, I meant to. It's just, well, I suppose I didn't want to upset you.'

'And now you do? What are you going on about?' asked Bea.

'I'm going to Tangier tomorrow for a week with Maya and her family.'

'Wow! That's great. Lucky you. I knew she'd be useful for something, one day.'

'So you're not upset?'

'No. No way. Anyway I'm going to France for three whole days.'

'With your family?' And then I added without even thinking, 'Or with Billy?'

Bea gawped at me. 'What made you say that?' I looked back at her. 'I mean how did you know? It was Mum,

49

wasn't it? She opened her big mouth and blurted it out to your mum. Knew she would. I'm sorry, Lily.'

'No, no, you've got it wrong. I saw the two of you together.'

'Where? When? How could you?'

'Through the window. Outside. Last night. It was sleeting. You looked like you were both having so much fun.'

'So,' she looked up at me with her big eyes whilst biting her lip, 'you're not actually cross with me?'

'No of course I'm not. Jealous? Definitely. Billy is the hottest guy in the whole of, well, this street and maybe even Battersea.' And we laughed and hugged like friends should. Then we did a little jumpy dance about the room before collapsing and swapping presents. We are so totally alike, and so totally different. We'd both got nail varnish for each other, but she got me black varnish and a packet of Black Jacks to turn my mouth a matching black, and I'd got her Jungle Red and some cherry sweets in the shape of lips that turned out to taste of washing powder.

'So, how was Christmas and Mr Taylor?' she said, offering me another sweet.

'No thanks. Sorry they're so disgusting – they looked so nice. Mr Taylor? Don't you mean Pat?'

We set out Monopoly and swapped our hideous

Christmas Day tales and made more Mr Taylor jokes. We discussed him and Dad and men for most of the game. Before we knew it, Bea was being summoned for dinner via my mum, on the phone to hers.

'Promise me one thing, Lily, just one thing?' she said, grasping me by the arms and shaking me with a real urgency.

'What? Yes, anything, OK.'

'You won't get kidnapped into the white slave trade,' she said, pinching my cheeks. 'A lovely girl like you could fetch a few camels in the right market.' We walked down the stairs, our arms entangled together.

'Ha ha. Thanks, I'll try not to. And you have fun in my favourite country with my favourite Billy. And don't you dare tell him you-know-what,' I shouted, running out of the front door and up the street after her. 'You haven't, have you?'

'What?' she shouted back.

'You haven't told Billy that I used to fancy him.'

And then I saw I was shouting right by his front door. I shrieked in horror.

'No, but you just did! Joking – he's away today!' I could still hear her laughing out of the darkness as I went back into the house.

Ah, Bea! You've got to love the scrappy little devil.

27th December – A Flight to Remember

I woke with dreams of kasbahs and white-sheeted, mysterious sheiks riding over deserts upon camels, and Mum shouting in strange tongues in my ear.

'C'mon Lily, they're going to be here in half an hour. Done your packing? Have you remembered those presents for Maya and her parents? Get into the shower whilst I make you some toast.'

'I had a bath last night,' I lied.

'OK, sure you won't smell too much? Get dressed. I'll take your bag down and make your breakfast.' And off she scuttled like Mrs Cottontail in *The Tale of Peter Rabbit*.

I dressed and packed a small bag with my book, diary, hairbrush, lip-gloss, cover-up, sunglasses and a few other essentials, like perfume and suncream and a snack or two. You couldn't be too careful in case of emergencies. I was dressed and polished, except for one thing – my shoes. Poppy had promised she'd put them back clean and de-sickified, but they weren't there. Well, I wasn't going without them. Mum would have to storm the enemy territory as I ate breakfast.

Ding Dong

'Mum, have you got them yet?' I shouted up. 'They're here, I have to go. I've got no shoes on.' Bay tugged my hand. 'No Bay, I can't wear your slippers – they don't fit.'

Bay is very sweet, but hardly the Brain of Britain.

'Maya!' I yelled, as I answered the door. 'God, I'm so excited. I just have to say goodbye to the animals.'

'Since when did you have pets?'

'I mean my family.' They were following me up the hallway, with my luggage and damp shoes.

'Thanks a lot, Poppy.'

'Yeah, well don't wake me up again for at least a week.'

'Not a problem. Tell Nick he can vomit on your shoes from now on, because you're never borrowing mine again.'

'Now, now, girls. Say goodbye nicely . . . They love each other really,' Mum said to Maya's parents, who had come to the door, saying all sorts of pointless platitudes about looking after me, as if I was a baby who'd never been away.

The chauffeur put my bag into the boot and I was about to get in the back when I realised I'd forgotten my coat. Just then Bay ran out of the house with it, all smiles, and I put it on and gave him a big hug, lifting him up. All right, I was slightly showing off because he was looking so cute.

'Now you be a good boy for Mama?' He nodded. 'Say hello to Maya and Maya's mummy and daddy.'

'Hello,' he said, and they cooed as he waved perfectly . . . and then farted so loudly he burst out giggling.

'Mum, take him, he's disgusting.'

I kissed her and she said, 'Phone when you get there. I've topped your phone up so you can text – if it works there.'

'Thanks, Mum.'

I got into the back of the nine-seater leather interior limo and we were off. 'Stop! My passport,' I suddenly shouted, and we reversed back.

And then finally we left. I'd escaped my family – annoying Bay, screaming Poppy and neurotic Mum – and I was going on an adventure. What could be better?

Rewards for Being Good

Maya and I weren't really able to talk in the car, not properly. Parents these days always seem to want to join in. So we played at being polite and talked about nice things. I wasn't about to tell Maya's parents about my lunatic parents and their Christmas row.

Finally we got through passport control and all the baggage/terrorist searches and we were sitting on the plane – in Business Class! None of that mixing with the riff-raff.

'I could get used to this,' I said, settling into my seat.

'What?' Maya replied, as if it was all totally normal – and it probably was for her. I wondered if she'd ever flown normal bucket class. Her parents were settled in on the other side of the aisle, her father reading the paper and her mother putting on a sleeping mask.

The air-hostesses started giving us things immediately. They gave us little boxes of chocolates and drinks – rewards for being good at sitting down, I expect. Then there were slippers and toothbrushes, and even menus to choose from for food and films. The plane was delayed, but I didn't mind. A man and an interesting-looking boy came through our section. They were obviously the reason for the delay because they were apologising profusely. The boy was so good-looking he made Billy seem ordinary. I guessed he was with his dad and – *zut alors!* – they seemed to be speaking *en français!*

'You know, Maya, Christmas suddenly seems to be looking up,' I said. 'There's a gorgeous-looking boy going through there.' He caught my eye and smiled, before disappearing into First Class. I settled back happily, smiling to myself.

'What's up with you and boys? It's always about boys, Lily. There are much more interesting things in the world. I wonder what movies they've got on?'

As the plane's engines started to gear up for the runway, I could feel my eyelids getting heavy, and before we'd even taken off I was asleep.

Up, Up, and Away

Oh Diary,
I have just woken up with a jolt and a snap. My forehead is
pinned to the aeroplane window. We are flying high above a
patchwork quilt of irregular green and brown fields, all
magically fitting together. I love this bit – everything in
miniature.

The plane rises and the land vanishes, as we're eaten by
a rain-spitting cloud. Then we fly above it into the infinite
blue. Beneath us, the clouds look like snowy hills made of
whisked egg whites. Maya is watching a fantasy movie next
to me, but it's nothing compared to this. It makes me think
anything might happen away from home. It makes me
believe in gods and heavens, golden chariots and angels'
wings, goddesses in trailing white dresses . . . I really want a
white goddess dress for the summer.

I am going to forget about the hideousness of Christmas,
Dad, Suzi, Mum and Pat. What a mess! But, thank God,
Maya's family is normal. I can relax. This is going to be a
real holiday without the stresses and strains of MY family
life. For the next week, dear diary, I promise you, I am
just going to have the best time, ever. It's Official.
Whatever Maya wants to do, we'll do, and we're NOT
going to argue. I learned stuff going on holiday with Bea to
Norfolk at half-term. I'm going to put my friend first,

however many gorgeous boys there are. I know this holiday is going to be so much fun.

Have just been to the loo and accidentally-on-purpose went through to see if I could see the French boy. I just wish he was on our holiday too, and not just on our plane. C'est la vie, eh!

CHAPTER FOUR

Nous sommes arrivés

27th December – Checking In, Check It Out

I took the chance to write down my first impressions as we drove from the airport into town (notes for future poems).

> *El Minzah, Tangier, Morocco, Africa, the world, the universe.*
> *Here in Morocco! Driving along the esplanade, Tangier, sea and waves, large and green, crowned with crashing foam; the beach windswept and barren, littered with rubbish. Windy but warm, the sun is shining. This is going to be such fun. Handwriting all over the place. Give up.*

'Hey, I can't wait to go swimming.' Maya's voice was heavy with sarcasm.

'Nobody goes swimming on the beach, honey, we have a pool for that,' Maya's mum, Nancy, explained to us helpfully, with her LA smile. (Why do all Americans have such perfect white teeth?)

We drove up a steep street and wound our way around the city until we were looking down on a mass of white and blue houses on cobbled pathways. The thin streets, threaded with mysterious shops, all go to make up what the driver told us was the famous kasbah.

Tangier is beautiful and strangely foreign. It looks French with its wide boulevards, Spanish with its orange trees and buildings, and yet Arabic with its people. It's also very noisy: there was the beeping of mopeds, the wailing of prayers over loudspeakers, the occasional bleat of a goat (getting on a bus!), taxis' horns, and shouting. Palm trees line the streets everywhere. Only the children seem to wear western clothes. The women wear long shapeless, coloured dresses, scarves over their heads and sometimes veils across their faces. The men wear shapeless dresses too, over trousers and shirts. Sometimes they have turbans wound round their heads. Screaming children ran after our long black sedan at the traffic lights. I felt like a popstar!

The car eventually stopped at the hotel steps and we climbed out. *Nous sommes arrivés!*

'Wow. You know, guys, this is one of the last great hotels,' said Maya's dad, Brett, his arms outstretched. 'In the old days everybody used to stay here – movie stars like Rita Hayworth, politicians, artists like Francis Bacon, Mick Jagger and Jerry Hall. It was an international city like Casablanca after the war.'

A brace of bellboys were picking our luggage out of the car. They were about our age and grinned at us cheekily. We passed two dignified moustachioed guards who stood either side of the hotel's front door, ancient speared weapons in hand, red cummerbunds on top of weird joined skirt-short-trouser things, and embroidered waistcoats, all matching their red fez hats, black tassels falling to one side. They looked like characters out of a Tintin book – the Twins in disguise.

'Wow, it's incredible and so – well, so foreign, isn't it?' I whispered to Maya.

'If you think this is weird you should try Dubai or Rajasthan in India. The palace hotels are outrageous,' Maya said back, nonchalantly.

'So this seems kind of normal to you?' I asked. I couldn't help but feel ordinary.

'No! I've never been to Morocco before, silly.'

We walked up the grand marble stairs and inside there was a treasure trove of Moroccan lamps and carpets, inlaid furniture and coloured glass. As we passed, people smiled and bowed, saying '*salaam*'.

'That's a kind of blessing people use to greet you,' I whispered to Maya. I had been reading my book about Tangier on the three-hour flight over.

A wide staircase beckoned us up. Ceremonial costumes stood in glass cases, whilst the sound of splashing water drew us through a panelled Moroccan tea-room, full of low tables and leather poufs, and out to a patio with a fountain.

Just Like Battersea, Not

As Maya's parents did all the boring bits of filling in paper and handing over passports, Maya and I set off to explore.

'Don't go far, girls, otherwise you won't know where your room is,' Maya's mum called after us, but we had already gone. We got into the white courtyard, trailed with bougainvillea (we have it around our doorway at home – a little bit of Battersea in Tangier, imagine that!) and through the side, past tall bushes full of white and blood-red dripping flowers, into the wide garden with a huge blue lagoon-like swimming pool, overhung with fuschia blossoms.

There was hardly anybody about. A few people were lying on the white wooden sun loungers that decorated the neat apple-green clipped lawn, sipping on drinks, basking in the last of the late sun. Still, it was more than warm enough for Maya and me, overdressed and fresh from freezing ol' Blighty that was overcast when we left.

'I love the magic of leaving one place with grey skies and arriving a few hours later in another with bright blue skies and sunshine. Hey, the sun looks like a yellow cough lozenge, stuck in the corner of the sky, doesn't it? I think I'm going to like it here.'

Maya wasn't listening to me. Her head nodded appreciation as she surveyed the scene. Maya's like that – she's quiet and considered, almost the opposite to Bea. She has a very dry sense of humour, too. Most people don't even know she's joking half the time, not even her parents. You have to look carefully for the mischief, a spark in her eye, because her voice and expression always remain seriously dead-pan. It doesn't help that she looks a lot like Wednesday, the daughter in *The Addams Family*. She dresses like her too, and her dark hair is always in two plaits either side of her pale face.

'Me too. Can't wait to go swimming,' she murmured.

'Yes, please. My sister bought me the hottest bikini for Christmas.'

'You see, Lily, you're always complaining about Poppy, but she gives you great presents. You don't appreciate your sister, I swear. I don't have any sisters to give me presents.'

'Oh, you poor little rich girl, Maya. I have a present for you,' I sung tunelessly.

She screwed up her nose at me.

'You know you can buy any bikini you like any time, but if you really feel so deprived, feel free to swap families with me.'

'Gee, thanks. We better go and find our room and see if the parents want anything. Let's go swimming before supper. I can't wait to dive in.'

'Maya, thanks so much for bringing me. This is so exciting,' I said, trying not to sound as totally bowled over as I was, because that would not be my normal sophisticated self!

We walked back inside, past a long wooden bar complete with a white-coated barman shaking a silver cocktail shaker. He smiled at us. Everyone seemed so friendly. I felt like I was in a movie.

When we got near to the reception desk I swore the hot French boy from the plane was standing there. This was like the best kind of film ever, with fantastic special effects. My stomach twisted and jumped, as if it had turned into a puppy.

It was definitely him! There was a god listening to my prayers! Thank you, God! The French boy was really standing there with his dad, and his dad was talking to Maya's mum and dad! This was almost unbearable, and too good to be true. As we approached they turned, smiled and introduced us.

'Hey girls, this is François. François is our good friend Olivier's son, and you'll never guess – they were on the same flight and we never collided. François is almost the same age as you two.'

'A little bit older I think, no?' Olivier said in one of those dreamy French accents that makes me want to emigrate immediately.

'Hi, I am François, I am fifteen. Very pleased to meet with you,' he said to us.

I was struck dumb, and stared blatantly at him.

Neither of us said a thing, so Maya's mum had to introduce us.

'This is Maya, our daughter, and this is her English friend, Lily. Of course you know we're living in Chelsea, London, now, Olivier. It's so great that we're all here at the same time. Is your wife coming?'

'Sadly not. Sabrine is having to work back in Paris, so François and I come away for our adventure together.'

'Well, that's just wonderful.' Nancy was overjoyed.

'Hello,' said Maya to François, pretending not to look at him. But he took her hand and held it to his lips and said, '*Enchanté*'. She was so shocked she just stared at him, her eyes wide.

'Gee, honey, isn't François cute, and so well mannered?' said Nancy.

'How do you do, François? *Bonjour*,' I said, going to shake his hand. He kissed my hand too and looked at me with such whirlpool toffee-brown eyes that I almost fainted when he whispered on to my hand, '*Enchanté*'. I was sure everybody had noticed that I'd melted into a putrid pink mushpot. I must have looked just like Mum's beetroot soup.

'Hey, we should have dinner together, or drinks or something – right, girls?' Maya's dad said. Brett was ever so jolly and friendly, but how could I eat near this boy? I'd have no appetite and nothing to say. I'd probably just stare at him until my eyes fell out and I stopped breathing.

We nodded dumbly.

'Well, here are your keys. They've taken your bags up already. Let's say we'll meet down in the bar over there at seven. Gives us all time to relax and freshen up.'

'OK, sweetie?' Nancy looked concerned. Maya had gone into a trance-like state.

'We thought if it was all right, we'd go for a swim,' I said.

'Sure, if you want to freeze your butts off. Just make sure you take a hot shower after.'

I didn't need a hot shower after meeting François – I needed a cold one.

Tangerine Dream

Our room was big, beautiful, ornate, opulently furnished, and mostly orange. It looked like a delicious juicy tangerine.

'Wow!' I leaped like a pancake on top of one of the two double beds. 'This is fantastic,' I said, because it was, and I knew in my heart that I had met the love of my life. Oh François – I had never been in such a state of bliss in my life.

'Hey, it's got a great view too,' said Maya opening up the French windows on to the balcony and leaning out for rather a long time.

'And what is the view, exactly?' I asked suspiciously, joining her. I saw right away. Two balconies on, sat François's dad. I wasn't stupid – François was either in the same room or just next-door.

'All I can say is, I'm not joining the French Resistance, that's for sure,' said Maya, in a way that frightened me. Her whole tone of voice had changed. Maya didn't like boys. She'd never seen the point of them. Why had I started to feel sick? I had a horrible feeling . . .

'You like François?' I asked.

'Oh my God, yes! And Lily, you must have seen the way he looks at me. I know this is going to be some amazing love affair. I'm, like, totally in love.'

'What? Maya, did I hear that?' This was so unlike Maya, I felt like I needed to pinch myself. This was too cruel to even acknowledge. What kind of game were the gods playing with us? I felt like a pawn in a game of chess and I was definitely losing.

'We could even end up together for ever. I mean, it all makes sense. Perfect beautiful sense.' She began to dance around the room in a strangely unhinged ballet manner. This was not the Maya I knew. She must have got swapped on the plane when I dozed off.

'It does? But you never like boys.' This was so wrong. Wrong and unfair.

'Yes. It's perfect, can't you see?' She was leaping and dancing around the room whilst chattering like a chipmunk, before finally collapsing in the empty bath, fully clothed and shod. 'Yes, of course it makes sense! I mean his dad's this famous French director who wants to move up a notch, François has been an actor since he was, like, ten, and my parents are producers. We can all make films together, for ever and ever. It's a marriage made in heaven.'

She'd obviously tipped over the edge into the land of Bonkers Mad. 'But you're only fourteen, and what are you going to be doing?' I felt my voice coming out striped with envy, and I couldn't help it.

'What do you mean? Are you being hostile, Lily?'

'Of course I'm not,' I said, desperately trying to control my jealousy, which was seeping out of every pore and jumping Grinch-like from my head.

She was right, it did make sense. Why were my parents

67

so selfish as to not be film producers? Why didn't they do anything useful that would bring me into contact with gorgeous French boys like François?

'No, I just meant that if François is acting, his dad is directing and your parents producing – what will you do on a film set?'

'Oh, I can do costumes, or better still, be François's personal dialogue coach to get rid of his cheesy French accent and teach him to speak properly. Do you think he makes it up? He sounds like a waiter. No one would understand him in the States.'

I tried not to weep out loud. I knew something would show in my face, so I buried it in my suitcase whilst pretending to look for my bikini and Maya's present. I knew it was right at the top of my case, just where I'd packed it. *Je suis désolée*, as François would have said if I'd bumped into him. I now said it to myself, not because I'd just bumped into somebody and was apologising; this time I was saying sorry – sorry for tripping up my own heart.

Swimming at a Time Like This?

'You still want to go swimming?' I swiftly changed the subject, to try and think of something else. 'Oh and here's your present. Happy Christmas, Maya.' I forced a smile, and held the package out.

'Swimming? Swimming! Lily, how can you think of swimming at a time like this? Or presents?' She must have been obsessed – she tossed it on to the table without opening it, her eyes glazed in wonderment. 'Now I know how you felt about Blake. I couldn't understand why you went so soppy and weird over him, why you wanted to travel all the way to Norfolk to see him. All I know is, I'd travel across the wilderness of Alaska if François was there at the other end.'

'Wow! That's love.'

'You know, I think it is. Lily, I've never felt this way before.' And then she began to cackle and laugh in a rather worryingly mad way. Was this how it was going to be for a whole week? I was never like this, was I?

'Hey, Maya, if we go for a swim he should be able to see you from his room. I bet you've got some wild bikini. Maybe he'll come and join us?'

'You're a lot smarter than you look sometimes, Lily. Good thinking.'

'Gosh, thanks, Maya,' I said, getting changed.

'And I've got this amazing swimsuit which is like a bikini except it's got this giant gold ring at the tummy that joins it up.'

'Let's see it. Wow! It's fantastic.'

'Are you sure? Mum bought it. Maybe I should wear

this white one? No, I'm too white – it'd look like I was naked.' She giggled disturbingly.

'The black swimsuit is good.'

'Or this blue one? Or the gold one? Is the gold one cool?' Maya just kept pulling more and more clothes out of her case, which was double the size of mine. She probably had twenty dresses in there, all with matching shoes, bags and swimwear.

'If we don't go soon, it'll be too late. And even if he doesn't come too, at least he'll see how amazing you look in a swimsuit.' I was standing there in a baggy dress over my bikini, flip flops, and a towel, waiting by the door, feeling like a frump.

Within a minute, Maya was dressed, running out of the door for the lift.

28th December – My, Oh Maya!

Dear Diary,
Maya is gaga smitten. All she talks about, when she isn't with him, is François – from first thing in the morning, until late into the night. I have never heard anyone go on about anyone else so much – let alone Maya, who doesn't like boys and never gives them a second thought. Suddenly it's, 'Isn't he cute when he crinkles his nose? Doesn't he have amazing hair, gorgeous eyes, the best the world's ever seen?' Blah,

blah, blah. Didn't meeting him just make the holiday ten million times better? And always, how glad she is to have me with her, as I could advise her.

I kept my counsel to myself. Shakespeare in Julius Caesar *said this is impossible for women, but it's not. If I can do it, anyone can. Seeing François all the time – last night, this morning at breakfast – was hard. But what could I say, when he looked at Maya as if she were a temple of gold? Maybe I imagined that smile he gave me, that* je ne sais quoi? *that had seemed to be so full of messages. And that look when he'd kissed my hand! If I hadn't made it up, I had read it badly wrong – so wrong! I had to forget about it and that was that. He was Maya's. Maya was the winner. I would try not to be a bad loser.*

Sheik Chic

The previous evening, at dinner, François's father had invited us all to some masked costume ball at a grand house up in the hills overlooking Tangier, for New Year's Eve. We hadn't bought fancy dress with us, so Maya's parents had given her a handful of cash and said we could go to the market and buy something. I reckoned I could probably put together a *Pirates of the Caribbean*-type outfit out of the clothes I'd brought with me, without too much trouble, but would that be grand enough for this sort of party? I had the boots and I had the dress to hitch up. Or perhaps I could wear my orange Fifties' ball gown that I'd bought in a charity shop in Norfolk at half-term with Bea, and make a mask out of cardboard and ribbon. But that wasn't grand enough for Maya.

'I'm going to buy a great outfit. I'm thinking more a princess-of-the-Caribbean look, being rescued by the sheik of Arabia from the pirates.' She giggled as she thought of François. 'Something spun in gold and feathers, a beaded mother-of-pearl bustier, something so amazing. This is such fun!'

'Yup. But Maya, we're not down the road from Oxford Street or Camden Market.'

'No, this is even better. We've got the whole of the large bazaar here. Let's go this afternoon and check it out with Mom and Dad. One more swim – beat you to the end.'

I had a feeling this was entirely for François's benefit. Maya is the least competitive person I know, but suddenly she was trying to beat me in swimming races. There was no contest, because I was really meant to be a fish. I'm more comfortable in the water than I am walking, and can beat most boys in races, let alone girls. Obviously I had to let Maya win, so that François could think that she was the best. Only when we weren't doing the silly racing thing could I swim properly.

My favourite stroke is butterfly – it feels for a moment

that you can defy gravity by lifting out of the water as gracefully as a dolphin tips its tail and flips its head. I like somersault diving and back-flip diving, but I couldn't do any of that – not when anyone else was around. I didn't want to seem like I was showing off, not after the first time, when Brett had remarked on how good I was and that maybe I should teach Maya how to dive better – in front of François.

'No, honestly, that was a fluke dive. Usually I'm rubbish, Maya's a much better swimmer than me,' I had white-lied, and that seemed to sort it. I felt as noble as anyone has the right to feel – building up someone else by putting themselves down.

'Well, I seem to always win when we race, but I don't think you're trying hard enough,' she had sweetly said, as if she didn't believe I could win. Did she not see my expression? Did she not remember the time at CampHappy when I'd swum across the lake twice, beating everyone? I had begun to doubt my sanity. Was I really fatter and uglier, stupider and clumsier, poorer and worse at swimming than Maya? I was beginning to feel less than my usual Liliness and it was, as my Granny 1 sometimes says, 'most discombobulating!'.

'You are so, so fast and good,' François had said and gazed glazily at Maya. The girl who never smiles had beamed back at him. Really it was wonderful and I knew

I should be glad for her, and I had to stop feeling that it wasn't fair.

I had had my chance with love with Blake, and after all, you couldn't be in love all the time – you wouldn't be able to do anything else.

I had things to do to distract me, costumes to create. Luckily, I had some money from Dad and my granny money. I changed half of it into dirham before we headed out to explore and felt like a millionaire knowing how much I was worth.

Tangier is a city with traffic and shops, crazy drivers and long lines of men sitting outside cafés drinking mint tea and coffee from glass cups. But some parts of it looked like it was from an ancient place, and others like a *Poirot* set – like the Cinema Rif near the roundabout with palm trees and a fountain and white curved Thirties' apartment blocks. The walk around didn't last long because Nancy suddenly screamed, freaked out by the crowds of people pushing round us.

'I don't think I can stand all these hustlers for a minute more. This is worse than Tunisia or India. Can't they leave us alone?'

Every other minute, people seemed to be at our elbows asking to be our guides, promising to show us the city for free just because they wanted us as their best friends. It was a little unbelievable. I mean, they didn't even know how crazy we were. How could they want us as their best friends when we might be evil and conniving, cruel and as merciless as pirates?

The trouble was that Nancy and Brett glinted like white diamonds and gold in the morning sun. How could they not attract hustlers around them? They shouted money in Chelsea, where they were surrounded by the rich. You couldn't blame the poor of Tangier for being unable to resist the challenge of asking for a little.

I was less sympathetic when a man, who must have been as old as twenty-five at least, started clucking and whispering in my ear, 'You be my girlfriend, eh?' I learned my lesson about keeping up with Maya. I was not ready to risk a life in the white slave trade by looking in shop windows. What would I have told Bea? I couldn't break my promise to her.

Sanctuary

The hotel was a sanctuary from the outside world. Nobody could follow us inside, which was why they had the spear-holders at the door. Nancy said she'd leave her jewellery in the hotel safe when we went out later, and that she would dress down. 'I'll just wear some old jeans and sneakers and a hat. They won't know me from Aunt Ada.'

After lunch by the pool, we lay about reading. Well, I actually lay about writing in my diary. Occasionally I looked up through the branches shading me and watched beautiful birds in myriad colours flying between the trees. But I had nobody to share this with. Maya was being far too busy gawping and giggling with François, and the worst thing about it all was, she couldn't even speak French!

Totally Bazaar

I don't know who Aunt Ada was, but if she went around looking like Maya's mum, she should have been arrested for crimes against fashion. She was hardly invisible when her jeans had Swarovski crystals bleeding out of the seams, her sneakers were silver with gold laces, and her hat was a big straw one with scarves flowing off it. I think the French would have a good word for it. Meanwhile in English, 'conspicuous' would do.

'Maya, I think if we're going to haggle for anything for the costumes, we should stay away from your mum,' I said as we walked down into the darkness of the kasbah that afternoon, with its myriad trail of tunnels lit up by the lights shining from the stalls.

'I know she looks gross – look at her shirt – but that's just Mom. Hey Mom, great sweatshirt.' She gave her a thumbs-up.

'Thanks, honey. If I'd known you were into leopard-print, I would've got you one too.'

Maya tried to stifle her hilarity.

'I just meant she looks too rich,' I whispered. 'They'll charge us a fortune for every fancy-dress thing. I've been reading my book and it says, "All shopkeepers like to haggle". They don't respect you if you don't negotiate the price.'

'I hate haggling. It seems so mean and trashy when you've got the money anyway.'

'It's part of their culture, honestly. They'll think you're trashy if you don't.'

Some of the lanes and tunnels had houses built on top of each other, like a medieval city; some were dug out into stalls or workshops. I was glad I had trainers on; the cobbles were really slippery and even the donkeys that walked past us were skidding with their full panniers, as flies buzzed around their eyes and mouths. Poor things! The further in we went, the darker it got as more of the streets became covered and narrower. The stalls began to open up after being closed for the midday siesta. The later it got, the more people flooded into the narrow streets buying food from the market vendors or filling the small shack-like outdoor cafés. Naked bulbs hung from the tin roofs as the light faded quickly into a dark blue-blackness. There were so many different smells. There was a general muskiness mixed with donkey poo, but each time we passed a stall where huge bundles of fresh mint lay, it was overpowered by the sweet smell of the mint. Cafés, thick with charcoal smoke and the sound of wailing singers from a TV or radio, sent out savoury fragrances of meaty kebabs. The nougat stall perfumed the air with its nutty sweetness. Small smiling girls carrying baskets of bread on their heads and trays of doughnuts straight from the bakers hurried past. And then there were the spice stalls . . .

'There's so much to see, I can hardly take it all in,' I said, looking at everything.

'Don't worry, you don't have to buy it all now. There's another massive outdoor market where we can go to see the snake charmers and magicians; the kasbah isn't about to close up shop in the next six days,' Brett informed me, chuckling. As I relaxed, Maya became unusually hyper, even manic.

'Oh my God, Mom, look at this – and that! Don't you think I should have this solid silver belt and sword? I should definitely have the gold slippers, and these earrings, and the shirt!' I stood back and watched her. What had got into her? 'François would love me in that.'

'Sir, is this your shop?' asked her dad.

A gentle, older, moustachioed man nodded.

'How much you want for the bunch of stuff my daughter wants?'

'Well this is a very ancient sword, hundreds of years

old. An antique. This was used in the war against the infidels . . .'

'OK, what's the price? We're kinda in a hurry.' I could see it was making them uncomfortable. They were more used to being served in Harvey Nichols than being told about what they'd already chosen. The sword looked too new to be antique – more likely it was made for the tourist market in a workshop.

'*Combien pour tout cela, monsieur?*' I asked in French.

'But you speak English?'

'*Oui, mais français aussi.*'

'*Très bien. Pas moins que dix mille dirham – un très bon prix, mademoiselle.*'

'*Dix dirham pour tout, sauf le sabre.*'

'*C'est toi qui tiens les cordons de la bourse?*' The shopkeeper looked amused and laughed.

'What are they saying?' asked Brett.

'I don't know, she's speaking French,' said Maya.

'*Bien sûr.*'

'*Tu exagères!*'

'*Mais c'est trop cher.*' I watched Maya and her parents stand and gawp at what I would like to think was my tremendous talent at *français*, but perhaps it was my nerve at butting in like that, that amazed them.

'*Mais non, les chaussures sont à deux mille, la chemise trois mille, les bijoux aussi* . . . No less than eighteen,' he said.

'*Non, douze.*'

'*Dix-sept.*'

'*Treize.*' I wasn't backing down.

He didn't say any more.

'OK *merci*,' I said, and started to walk away, hoping the others realised as I gesticulated to them, they were supposed to follow. They didn't.

'Hey, let's just give the guy what he wants, and forget it.' Maya had spoiled the whole thing, and as the shopkeeper took the money, he had a dejected look on his face.

'*C'est comme ça*,' I said, and he beckoned me over.

'*Pour toi*,' he said. In my hands he put a beautiful amber beaded bracelet. He smiled at me and put his hands together and nodded his head and said something about Allah in Arabic. Somehow not all had been lost.

'That was great French you were speaking,' said Maya's mum, smiling. 'I wish Maya could speak French. Hey Maya, maybe you can get François to help you with your French.'

'Oh Mom, I think it's more important I help him with his English first. Everybody needs to speak English. Besides, there's lots of time.' She ran up to me then and asked, 'Lily, what was it with you and that old guy? You didn't have to haggle – Dad has the dough. It doesn't matter.'

Maya obviously didn't understand what I'd said about

it being a matter of pride for the shopkeeper – the difference between striking a bargain with a friend and not even bothering to look at the person you buy something from in a store. It's about exchanging friendship and time, not just goods; everything is on a personal level of honour in Morocco. 'Good manners are one of the most important things to Moroccans, it says here.' I pointed to my guidebook. 'You should always treat everyone with respect. Under Allah's eyes, we are all equal.'

'But some of us are more "equal" than others, right hon?' Brett laughed with Nancy at his joke.

We walked down the pebbled walkways. Bashed and broken beggars lined the street; some were limbless on trolleys, others were children with crutches, holding out metal cups for coins.

'Yeah, so how come there are so many beggars in the streets, if everyone's equal.' Maya's cynicism came leaking out.

'I didn't mean that. But look – everyone's putting money in the cups when they pass. It's not like London, where everyone just tries to ignore beggars. Look – the man from the café there just gave that child a plate of food. He didn't have to do that.'

'This is a weird country. Look at the kids with mud in their hair and that woman with tattoos on her face. It's definitely weirder than those other places where the men wear dresses.'

'The tattoos are henna, a semi-permanent red dye they use to colour their hair and decorate their skin. I think it's pretty,' I replied.

'Dad,' Maya called, 'can I have some money to give to the beggar? The custom is you're not supposed to pass them without putting a coin in their cup, otherwise it's, like, really bad luck, Lily says.'

'Sure, honey, as long as they don't all want some – right, Nancy? Otherwise they'll think we're billionaires.' And he laughed again, but I wasn't quite sure why.

CHAPTER FIVE
Cheap at the Price

29th December — No Good, Double-Crossing Gal

A light knock at the door woke me. *'Bonjour mesdemoiselles, le petit-déjeuner pour vous.'* And a pretty woman entered in her white-and-pink maid's outfit, carrying a tray. She put it on the table and opened the curtains before leaving. Hot chocolate, fresh orange juice, croissants, warm rolls, jam and fresh flowers; what more does anyone need first thing in the morning – or last thing at night?

Maya and I had decided the night before that we would fill in the breakfast request list and have our breakfast on the balcony – just the two of us. I wondered if this meant she was calming down, and wasn't so madly obsessed with François as I'd first thought. I hoped so – it would make it a lot easier for me. I was finding it hard not to show my feelings for François. I kept trying not to think about how gorgeous he was, and channelling all my energy into having a good time and designing the best outfit ever for the fancy-dress party on New Year's Eve.

Another bright-blue-sky day, lay before us! All slightly different from the usual way I get woken up by Bay, with his plastic sword prodded up my nose, before I have to get my own breakfast.

'Look how lovely it is again, Maya. Bet it's raining in London.' I laughed smugly, caught up in the luxury. 'This must be the best hotel in the world. Do you think it is?' I asked, knowing that she had that much more experience. When she didn't answer, I wondered if she was still asleep.

'Come on, sleepy head.' I threw a pillow at Maya's bed. Nothing happened. 'You haven't died in the night from consuming such vast quantities of pudding, have you?' (The hotel restaurant was fantastic, with both a Moroccan menu and a French one. We were sticking to the French, especially with puddings. Maya had done herself proud last night with a *millefeuille* of pastry stickiness, followed by a *crème brûlée*.)

There was no answer from her bed, so I jumped out of mine and on to hers. There was nothing there except the sheets and pillows that she'd left in her usual scrambled mess. I assumed she was in the bathroom, so I politely knocked on the door. Nothing. I opened it. Maya had gone without even leaving a note.

I sat on the loo and thought, 'That no good, double-crossing gal'. Then I brushed my teeth and thought some more, and had an extra think, whilst washing my face and brushing my hair. All of which was interrupted when I looked in the mirror and wished I wasn't quite so pudding-faced, curly-haired or knobbly-thighed; if I wasn't, maybe I would be with François.

'That is a totally rubbish thought. Only a rubbish man who lived in a rubbish bin, would think of that,' I said loudly to the mirror, to make sure that I heard it properly, not just as a passing thought. I knew how I looked had no bearing on what had happened – that was stupid. Things happen, they just do, to teach you stuff about who you are and what you can do with your life. Mirrors are a great distraction from thinking. In fact Granny 2 once told me that she was bought up by her granny with no mirrors at all in the whole house because vanity was one way the devil could creep into your soul.

Breakfast Blues

Thinking about devils, I went towards the balcony, and as I opened the French windows all suspicions were verified. I could practically get a job on *CSI* or as a young, glamorous Miss Marple. There, by the pool, were François and Maya, eating breakfast together like two little doves cooing over each other. Puke. The cooing seemed to enter the room, making me feel truly sick.

Still, I wasn't going to let that ruin my appetite. I moved the tray on to the outside table, put my hair up with a pencil in a bun on top of my head (*très chic mademoiselle!*) and I sat down to eat my two breakfasts. A soft fresh breeze ruffled the hair on my arms. I shivered in the early cool of the day; it was cold out of the sun. In the far distance I could see the harbour with a white ship sailing in on a green sea. A faraway wailing of voices calling people to prayer carried on the wind. Closer by, I could hear the rough sweep of the pool boy's brush as he cleared leaves from around the pool, and the busy morning chatter of birds. I pretended not to hear the most obvious noise – them.

I put my lips to the thick, creamy, to-die-for hot chocolate. I could drink it for ever without feeling sick. The orange juice was so fresh and, well, orange, that it must have been made from fruit which had just been picked off the trees. I could see the trees from the balcony – the hotel kept their own orange, lemon and grapefruit groves. Later, I would go for a walk and investigate them by myself. If Maya and François wanted time alone, I would give it to them in bucketfuls. I wasn't going to whinge to be included. I had books, my diary, the swimming pool (except they were there) . . . I had even brought my sketchbook and watercolours with me. I could paint the same view that Matisse had once painted of the harbour with the minaret tower, a print of which was on the loo wall at home. In short, I was a very busy person who didn't need others to dictate agendas to me. The day would soon pass. Already it was almost – I looked at my watch – only eight o'clock? By the time I was dressed and showered and organised I figured it would be nine.

Actually it took until eight-thirty. I tried to paint but I didn't have the concentration. And I thought time was supposed to race by when you were having fun.

Too Pretty for Politics

I turned on the TV and watched Sky News and thought about the international situation. Everyone should try to think more internationally, what with global warming and such, but it wasn't long before I was defeated by the politicians – they were just too ugly to look at. Why do they make them so ugly? What comes first – you're so ugly you go into politics, or you go into politics and it makes you ugly? Interesting. Must suggest politics as a career move to Poppy.

I went to get the last croissant that was crying out 'Eat

87

me, eat me' from the balcony. I was wearing my favourite blue-and-white sailor sundress with my cute red espadrilles tied up my legs, and my hair was in a ponytail. I looked around when I heard a 'Yoohoo!' coming from the garden.

'Hey, Lily, why don't you come down. François and I —'

'Shhh!' said someone from another hotel window.

'Later,' I called back with a surprised look, as if I hadn't known they were there all along. No one was out in the gardens except for them and the pool boy, now putting out the sunbeds. How could I not have seen them?

First Sign of Madness

I didn't want to be like Bea had been, when I'd wanted to spend time with my boyfriend Blake, when we were staying with his parents in their mansion in Norfolk. She never wanted to leave us alone. After all, I wasn't like Bea. I put on some more lip-gloss (the problem is it tastes too nice and I always lick it off – I wonder how many kilos I swallow a year?) and found my sunglasses.

'I like being on my own, don't I, Lily?' I said to the mirror, doing some hilarious posing. 'Yes, you do, Lily, and may I say just how particularly gorgeous you are looking today?' . . . 'Why thank you, you're looking pretty cute yourself,' I replied to my reflection, before I realised that talking to yourself was the first sign of madness.

'Who are you talking to, Lily?' asked Maya, bursting into the room with François right behind her. I was suddenly frantically tidying up bras and knickers off the floor, and stuffing them into my bed. 'Oh nothing, just reciting poetry.'

'Huh. You know poetry?' said François. 'You know Rimbaud?'

'Yes. I mean I've read him and Flaubert,' I said, crossing my fingers behind my back because I hadn't actually, but I had heard of Rimbaud, the famous drunken French poet who died at a tragically young age.

'*Je me suis baigné dans le Poème De la Mer . . .*' François suddenly spurted out, throwing his hands to the ceiling dramatically.

'Wow!' I said. 'Did he really say, I have bathed in the poem of the sea?'

'Hey you guys, no time for that. I was trying to tell you to come down because we're leaving in five minutes – for the camel market that happens, like, once in a blue moon.'

'Oh right, well, I'm ready. Let me just grab my bag, jacket and glasses.'

'This is what Lily always does,' Maya whispered to François.

'What do I always do?'

'This. Say you're ready and then buzz around for

another ten minutes before you leave. Your glasses are on your head.'

François laughed.

Maya was being a traitor to the female cause. I wish I'd given her *The Female Eunuch* for Christmas, or a CCTV system so that I could record her behaviour and show it back to her. She hadn't even bothered to open her present from me, or give me mine; maybe I'd swap it for some nougat to keep her teeth stuck together.

'I do not. OK, sometimes I do, but count to ten and I'm ready. *Me voici!*' François kept laughing, Maya joined in, and finally I had to pretend to think it funny as well, even when I didn't.

How is it that out of two perfectly nice separate people, couples can sometimes make the most horribly irritating combination?

Or maybe it was the bitter memory of being like that myself with Blake and Bea in Norfolk. Oh it tasted like honey, but honey made by wasps not bees, into a bitter cough medicine.

A Land of Sand

All of us drove out of Tangier together in a huge hired 4x4, with Olivier at the wheel. The adults were immersed in their adult conversation, whilst Maya and François whispered and giggled together. I sat and stared out of the window as the road took us out into the desert. There was the occasional palm tree, and the odd shack covered in Pepsi and Coke signs, which seemed to be in the middle of nowhere selling snacks to no one. Usually I am very against gas-guzzling Land Rovers, but they were invented for a reason, and the reason was the road we were on, which was distinctly dodgy and became more like a track the further we went – not that anyone else noticed and so I had no one to discuss it with.

There weren't even many cars on the road. The ones that were had goods piled high on top of their roofs, or were joyfully and dangerously overtaking us. In the distance behind us the mountains were disappearing into the clouds.

'I wonder if those are the Rif or the Atlas Mountains, over there?' I asked nobody in particular, and nobody in particular answered me back. The grown-ups were still too busy talking about films and business deals, just as they had the night before. Maya and François were lost in their own language, which now seemed to involve much prodding and tweaking of each other's noses, ears, etc., followed by much giggling. I couldn't see the joke myself. I had obviously lost my sense of humour. Ha ha hilarious.

Now I knew how Bea had felt. I suppose the word is lonely. I hate that word, but I couldn't think of another.

At least if I was with Poppy we'd be arguing. I fished out my mobile, and tried to send a text to Bea.

To Bea – Wish you were here! It is BEA-utiful!

A little symbol flashed – no signal, damn and blast. Maybe we were too far out of Tangier.

We seemed to drive on for ever. Spotting my first camel gave me something to look at, and there wasn't just one – there were six of them, all laden with rugs and boxes and bags, with men riding between the hump and the neck in a graceful lolloping gait, coloured turbans upon their heads. It was like a scene out of one of Mum's favourite old films, *Lawrence of Arabia*; they'd made us watch it in history class last year. I remembered coming home from school and telling Mum, and having to listen to her getting all excited over Peter Tool or whoever he was, and how sexy he was with his cornflower blue eyes. I'd said they were probably digitally enhanced and brown in real life. She'd got furious, and said things weren't enhanced in those days, not even boobs!

It's strange when you think of all the things that hadn't been invented when our parents were our age. They didn't even have mountain bikes or computers, or video recorders, let alone DVDs, and they had to go to cinemas if they wanted to see films because there were no film channels. It must have been the same for Brett, Nancy and Olivier.

It was only once I'd stopped listening to the snippets of other people's conversations and started to have the ones in my head that I forgot about my loneliness. Thinking made me feel much cheerier. Before I knew it, we were parking the car and getting out amidst a mass of dust and reek of camel dung.

The market was an amazing sight. It was out in the middle of the desert with no buildings around. The stalls were all piled high with spices, melons and vegetables. But at the centre of it all were the camels. There were hundreds of people milling about the stalls. The best-dressed women wore stripes of blue paint down their faces, straw hats as wide as tractor wheels upon their heads, and striped coloured blankets wrapped about their waists. All the women had amazing henna tattoos over their faces and hands. And quite a few older women and men didn't have teeth when they smiled. Slightly scary. 'Hey, Maya, these must be the Berbers that live up in the Rif mountains and come down to sell what they grow in the markets.'

Children were surrounding us, repeating *'un dirham'*, but as we walked amongst the mass of people, they dispersed. Olivier got out a camera and started to take pictures – it was obvious that people didn't appreciate it as they waved their arms, shook their heads, and turned away.

'Why don't they want me to take their pictures? I suppose they want money. Everything is about money here!' he said.

'Some people are superstitious. They think that when you take their photograph you're stealing a part of their soul,' I said, repeating part of the book that Mr Taylor had given me. 'It kind of makes sense in a way.'

'You know so much about this place. Are you sure you're not native?' Maya laughed, prodding me.

'It's called knowledge. It happens, when you gather information and read lots of books, Maya.'

'What's a book again, Lily?' she said, pretending to be dumb, whilst batting her eyelashes at François.

'Good question. In French it's *un livre*. I'm glad you're showing an interest. I must teach you to read one day – you'd like it,' I joked back.

'But Lily, you are joking always. This is ridiculous, what you say! If it were true, movie stars and models would have no souls left,' said François, and his father laughed.

So that's why they seem so ditzy in interviews, I thought, but knew it was best *fermer la bouche*.

Maya jumped in. 'You know, François, I wouldn't be at all surprised.' But then she spoiled it all by giggling hysterically whilst running away from him screaming, 'No! Keep away from me, beast,' but meaning the opposite. That girl was starting to give the word 'no' a bad reputation.

'Oh you are teasing me again, you are – 'ow you say – a wicked girl.' And he chased her.

Bum, bum, bum, as Bea and I are fond of saying, when things at home aren't quite as they should be. I admitted I was jealous and I could tell you it was not a happy feeling. Alone, without even my family, and in a strange country – I was not happy at all. The only beasts making eyes at me had great long eyelashes, were smelly and hairy and looked like camels. I walked among the stalls. At last, I could smell something other than camel – cinnamon and cardamon, cumin, coriander and cloves, wafted into my nostrils; the smells of foreign lands and imaginary tales. We were actually in the middle of the ancient spice route; in medieval times, spices were as precious as gold.

'Hey, stick together guys, we don't want you getting lost,' Brett shouted out.

I ran to keep up with them, but the slow drift of the crowds rubbing close together, and the rising waves of Arabic songs and sounds, made it hard and confusing. I stopped to buy some piratey hoop earrings and when I turned around everyone had disappeared. I began to feel a little panicky. How would I ever get back to the hotel if they left without me? I scoured the crowds and finally I caught sight of what I thought was François's blond head standing out from the thousands of dark-haired, or covered, ones. I ran towards it, snaking through the people. '*Pardon*,' I said, not knowing if they understood me or not, as I raced through the jelabahs and found myself next to the blond head of Olivier.

'Hi, I seem to have lost François and Maya,' I said, smiling nervously. Though we had had dinner together I didn't feel relaxed with him, knowing him even less than Maya's parents.

He was haggling with a Moroccan man. He turned and winked at me. I smiled politely and waited for them to finish, rather than risk getting lost again.

'*Tu comprends?* Did you understand? Maya said you speak French,' Olivier said to me.

'*Je parle français, mais lentement.*'

'So you did not understand what we said then?'

'*Non.*'

'So, Lily, it seems he would like to buy you for eight camels. What do you say? Pretty good, huh?' The expression on my face, filled with dread and horror, seemed to make Olivier laugh so loudly it attracted François, Maya, her parents, and a crowd.

'Hey, what's going on?' Brett asked.

'We could make ourselves a healthy profit. This man here wants to buy Lily in exchange for eight camels –

96

good, huh? Lily doesn't look impressed. How many do you think you are worth? Ten?'

'*Dix mille chameaux, pas moins!*' And everybody burst out laughing including my prospective owner. I, however, just like Queen Victoria, was NOT amused.

'Oh, don't be so sensitive. Imagine – you could live the romantic life of a nomad,' said Maya. 'And I'm sure he'd look after you.' They all laughed again.

'Well, you sell yourself into the white slave trade, if you like it so much. Actually, you'd probably have to pay *them* the camels to get them to take you.'

I was upset and stomped off back to the car. I was suddenly frightened by everything – the crowds, the heat, the smells, but most of all the feeling of loneliness – like no one else was on my side.

Why do some people think everything is so ha ha hilarious when it comes to teasing? Well, I don't call it teasing – I call it bullying. I wished Mum was there; even Poppy would have been better. I bet even Dad wouldn't have sold me for only eight measly camels.

Alone Again

'Oh, stop sulking,' said Maya, as sensitively as a hammer.

Ooh, I could've lashed her with a few of the occasions when we were at camp together in the summer and she had got homesick after two hours, let alone two days.

Had I said 'stop sulking' then? No I hadn't. I had tried to dissuade her from going home, and I hadn't been mean or laughed at her – I had tried to make her laugh and be her friend.

By the time we got back it had started to rain. François and Maya lamely tried to convince me that they wanted me to play table tennis with them. I had no problem saying no. 'Don't worry, I'm fine. You two play – I want to swim. I'll see you later.' I left them to it.

I bet Bea and Billy together would have been nicer to me.

Wet Swims

There is something beautiful about swimming in rain in hot countries. Being surrounded by water makes you feel strangely warmer than if the sun was out, especially when you get out to dive. Of course, nobody else was out by the pool so I dived as well as I could without worrying that my bikini top or bottoms would fall down (why do they always do that?), and swam, jumped and rolled around in the pool like an otter, until I felt my fingers begin to crease like old prunes, and a shiver cross the top of my skin. I got out and ran under the balcony where I'd left my wrap and flip flops to keep dry, and then I thought I might as well explore the orange and lemon groves – it was only a light rain. A sign was on the path saying in

French and English that guests should not go further than that point, but the trees were so beautiful – what harm could I do? They were glowing like an oil painting. Mum would've been in paradise. I was just about to pull an orange off the tree, when I heard a noise of rustling leaves by my feet. I looked down, screamed and ran. I have never run so fast in all my life in flip flops. I have never been so terrified. I got back inside the hotel and the first person I saw was the barman who always served us.

'Ça va, mademoiselle?'

It was no time to speak French. I reverted to my natural emergency tongue. 'Muhammed! There are scorpions out there! I just saw one.'

'No, not by the pool? Are you stung?'

'No, I was under the orange trees. It was a real live scorpion and it was running after me!' I was shivering.

'No? They stay where it is dry under the stones, and trees – that's why there is the notice. This is Morocco. Of course there are scorpions.' He then began to chuckle. 'I make you a hot drink and tell you a funny story, but first you get dry.'

I could understand why Muhammed was laughing at me. I felt pretty, pretty dumb! I had a warm shower and dressed in jeans, and went back downstairs with my diary. He made me a beautiful glass of sweet-scented mint tea as I sat up on a high bar stool. It tasted as good as it smelled.

'Why are you alone? A pretty girl like you should not be alone. Where are your friends?'

'Oh, they're playing games together. It's all right – I like being alone. My mobile phone doesn't seem to work here. There's no signal. I just wish I could speak to my mum or send her an email.'

'You can. The computer room is just upstairs to the left.'

'Wow, can anyone use it? I mean, does it cost much?'

'It is free for the guests.'

'Great. Keep my tea, I'll be back.'

'What about the story of the scorpions?' he called after me, but I had gone.

Safe

Subject: Still alive

Dear Mum,

Sorry I've not spoken to you. Did you get my message on the answerphone?

There is so much to tell you about Morocco. Tangier is beautiful. It looks like that book you have about Dufy – or is it Matisse? – all palm trees and ocean views through balcony railings, and completely white houses with roof terraces. Luckily, they speak quite a bit of French so I've been practising lots. And there's a French film-director friend of Maya's parents here with his son,

François. Maya is madly in love with him (vomit). The hotel is beautiful. I miss you. And Bay. And sometimes I even wish Poppy were here. Hope you have made it up with Pat. I don't mind him really, as long as you are happy.

Love Lily XXXXXXX

PS Has Dad said sorry yet for trying to burn our house down?

I decided to write a few more emails. It stopped me thinking about what was happening in the hotel. I decided that I liked my family more than other people's when I was away, however much I complained about them. I could also write to Bea and tell her things that were too frightening for Mum, like the scorpion incident. It's not a good idea to scare parents when they are too far away to do anything but worry and shout, 'Come home this minute,' over the phone.

Subject: Tangerine

Dear Bea,

I am so happy you are with Billy. Just writing that makes me feel happy for you – after all, it is a great combination of people, plus you are the same height, which must be useful, so you don't have to bend down to speak to each other.

Tangier is brilliant. It is really different, like being in a foreign film, like *Casablanca* (another city in Morocco, strange but true). The men wear long robes, turbans and all have moustaches – crazy, huh? Do you think it will ever catch on in England, with Billy? Imagine kissing a man with a moustache. It would be like having a toothbrush shoved in your mouth. Handy, as long as he didn't mind you adding toothpaste to it before you snogged. Could be quite messy.

Outside of the hotel, it is actually quite dangerous. I almost got sold into the white slave trade for eight camels this morning; I said I wouldn't go for under ten thousand camels, then I escaped. I mean if you don't keep your basic value up, who will? Also, just had a death-defying moment outsmarting the claws of a deadly scorpion. Am almost Supergirl. I wonder if they have ever thought of having a female James Bond. Back to the mint tea.

Shoukran for being my mate, and all that . . . Catch up back home, eh? Promise I won't investigate the white slave trade without you.

TTFN (TaTa For Now)

Lily XXXXXXXXXXXXXXXXXX

PS If you come from Tangier, you are a Tangerine!

I wrote a brief thank-you note to Dad, but it was pretty dull and very short and messy, a bit like Bay. Plus I thought he should be writing to me and apologising for his awful behaviour on Christmas Day. In fact, if I were him, I'd probably have already died from the embarrassment of behaving like that. I think parents have an inside memory wiper like an instant shaken Etch-a-sketch of the brain. But then I was almost cheered up when I saw one golden message in my inbox from Granny 1 in New Zealand.

It was lovely getting a message from Granny. It made me feel all hot-chocolate-warm inside (which is a v good feeling, since they discovered that hot chocolate's good for the brain).

When I looked at my watch I saw it was after six – later than I thought. I supposed I should find Maya and François, or I could go and write in my diary.

I walked out of the computer room to be greeted by the noise of Americanese, as I call a few Americans all squabbling at once. The noise rose up to the mezzanine floor where I was, so I went to look over the balcony and investigate. It was Maya's mum and dad, loudly gesticulating at the poor man at the desk.

'I thought there were guards here. Has no one seen her? How could she get out without anyone seeing? She might be anywhere.'

'She could've been kidnapped. What are we going to do?'

'We are busy asking all the staff. When was the last time she was with you?' asked the man at reception.

'Lunchtime . . .'

'When was the last . . .?' was all I needed to hear before

I ran headlong down the stairs. They obviously didn't know that Maya had gone off to the games room with François. I had to tell them and save the day. But then, I hadn't seen Maya for hours. Maybe she'd vanished.

'She was playing ping pong with François,' I shouted out. It was only when I got closer I realised.

'It's Lily!' they replied as if *I'd* been missing.

'Yes?'

'Oh Lily, there you are!' said Maya, who was hidden in front of the group by her dad. 'Where have you been? We thought you'd disappeared. We ransacked the hotel. We've all been worried crazy about you. You weren't out in the pool.'

'We were about to call the police. You must tell people where you are!' Maya's mum added.

'You said you were going swimming, *non?*' asked François.

A sea of faces stared at me expectantly.

'Sorry. Yes, I went swimming and I was just in the computer room, emailing my mum. What's going on?'

'Well, at least you're safe. We were just very worried, Lily,' said Brett, the voice of reason, followed by Nancy's hysteria.

'Crazy worried, after the camel market, and you being all upset. We just didn't know what had happened to you. Now don't you go running off again, you hear me? What would I tell your mother? I can't be responsible for you if you're going to behave so irresponsibly.'

Suddenly from feeling so cheered up, I felt like I'd just slaughtered half the population and was a very bad person indeed. I wouldn't be surprised if they sent me back on the first available flight. Right at that moment I wouldn't have minded. If I thought my mum was neurotic, Maya's was a whole new ballgame.

'Maya and François are under strict instructions not to leave you alone,' said Brett. I grimaced at my fate. Being alone isn't that bad. In fact it's a lot better than being next to a couple of drooling, lemur-eyed lovebirds. 'Now all of you better get dressed quickly. We're off to a belly-dancing nightclub for dinner. We'll meet in the bar in fifteen minutes, OK guys? Now don't go getting lost.'

'Sure, Dad.'

'Of course,' I replied. 'Sorry, I made people worry,' I said sheepishly, then trailed upstairs after love's young dream, wishing I was back home.

Dear Diary,

It's eleven p.m. and the sky is a beautiful blue with a stamped-on crescent moon. We've just come back from the most wonderful night! Maya has passed out from all the drama and disappointment that I wasn't missing in action. (Couldn't they just have asked Muhammed, the barman?)

I got dressed to go out to dinner with Maya sitting watching me. There is nothing that makes me so indecisive as getting dressed with someone looking at me. Luckily, I didn't have much choice with only three dresses, and one of those is an orange ball gown, so I put the warmer one on because it's so cold at night. Finally Maya asked what had happened to me in a bored way, and I told her the boring truth, but left out the scorpion (I didn't need hysteria, with extra hysterical topping). They had apparently left ping pong to go and 'play cards' in François's room. Maya said, 'Hey, sorry if we kinda left you outta things, it's just that I can see you, like, whenever we're in London, and François is going back to Paris soon.' I told her not to worry. I was fine alone.

And I am fine. It's weird how getting in touch with Bea and Mum, and the email from Gran, had made me feel a million times better. It's like knowing I still have my old teddy, even though I don't have him in my bed. Curieux!

Dinner was in a place called Hammadi's in the kasbah. A secret doorway led into a harem. We sat on the floor and ate our first Moroccan meal – sweet flaky pigeon pie followed by a massive meat stew called a tagine. At least we didn't have to eat sheep's eyeballs. Gross! There were acrobats and tray-balancing dancers, a magician that ate a glass and swallowed fire, and real live belly dancers with jewels in their belly buttons, their stomachs wobbling like giant jellies. But is it really sexy? François said it was, and when Maya was in the loo he asked me if I could belly dance as he'd 'like to watch'. So why do I feel guilty? François is gorgeous, but there's nothing to be done about it. But should I be learning how to belly dance if I want a boyfriend?

A Moroccan band played weird instruments as they sat cross-legged on the floor. It was amazingly dark and magical, and the music was hypnotic. It reminded me of a scene in an old James Bond film. I might do a Moroccan night for Mum when I get back. I could train Bay up to be a belly dancer. He'd be grateful later on that I'd taught him a skill.

Maya did try to be a bit more Lily-friendly and I tried too. I know I can be a bit ratty when I feel someone's not being my bestest friend. It was a good night and it was especially hilarious when Maya's dad started dancing with the belly dancer, and François's dad said they were usually boys, not girls! Maya's mum was in hysterics. We all were, except poor old Maya's dad, who stumbled back to the table sweating, his ponytail flopping, and asking, 'So what's the big joke, guys?' But the funniest thing was when François smeared red stuff all over his pie, thinking it was ketchup, whereas in fact it was harissa, a concentrated chilli paste. He howled, thinking his face was on fire. The waiter just managed to stop him drinking water (it makes it worse) and made him eat a basket of bread. I almost felt sorry for him. Even Maya was laughing. Poor François. I would've kissed him better if he wasn't Maya's . . . Luckily my willpower is as strong as steel . . .

Today just proved to me that, even if you think you're sometimes not wanted, you'll always be missed.

CHAPTER SIX

Looking Down and Looking Up

30th December – Blue and Green

I was standing on the edge of a cliff, high above Tangier. The tall, square, white lighthouse of Cap Spartel sat smartly in its flower-filled gardens behind us. The sky was that sweet baby-blue with small, fat clouds dotted on it. I thought how good it would be as wallpaper for my ceiling back home in my room, so I could lie on my back and dream I was somewhere else. It is always a good idea to have several escape routes from my family – books, movies, dreams, the front door . . . The sun was hot and my neck was prickling in the heat. In front of us was one of the most amazing things I think I'd ever seen.

'Just how is that possible?' I asked Maya.

'Don't ask me. François?'

'*Je ne sais pas.* I don't know.'

Somehow, the sea was divided in half, as far as you could see from where we were standing, above the Caves of Hercules. One half – the Atlantic half – was a glassy azure-green, but definitely green. The other half was the Mediterranean and a deep beautiful blue, and not a bluey-green. There was not even a bit in the middle where they met where it was kind of greeny-blue. The white line that you could see way out into the horizon was where one sea was fighting the other, creating a mane of white sea foam, as if mythical horses were charging away from the coast and into the sun in some giant magical race.

'It's so nice smelling fresh sea air away from the town. What's the Hercules sign down there about?' Nancy asked me. I had almost become an official guide.

'Apparently it's where Hercules lived a zillion million years ago. It's the Hercules Grotto,' I said knowledgeably, reading straight from my guidebook. I liked Nancy and Brett, but I didn't understand the way they thought. I wondered if it was because they were so very rich that they expected everybody to do and know everything for them.

'But he was just a myth, right? And if he was a myth how could he have lived there?' asked François.

'François, do you know nothing?' said his dad. 'Myths are stories taken from real life. Here we are surrounded by

Roman and Phoenician ruins. You always quote poetry, but you should read more, François. Knowledge comes from books.' Suddenly my father started to look rather nice in comparison. At least he never showed me up as stupid in public. 'Oh Lily, have you seen? There are some of your favourite animals down there.' Olivier laughed and I ignored his rudeness. I knew he was pointing at the camels which tourists could sit on to have their pictures taken. 'Don't the children want a camel ride?'

'I want a photograph of me on the camel, Papa,' said François, obviously regressing into a baby after being told off. So we walked down the path ahead of the grown-ups.

'Ah, look how cute the camels are, François. All pretty with their coloured bridles and reins.' This showed a new sentimental side to Maya that I never knew existed. Love does strange things to people. Next thing I knew, she'd be cooing over babies.

'I want eyelashes like theirs, and I bet they don't even use mascara,' I joked to Maya. 'Imagine, you'd save a fortune with just one pair of camel lashes.'

'But imagine if you had to have those teeth!' she replied. 'You'd be permanently at the orthodontist.' We laughed.

'Is make-up all you silly girls think about?' said François, dismissively.

'No, but have you ever tried putting psychology on your eyes? Actually, there is that make-up called Philosophy.'

'Ouch,' he screamed back.

'What? I didn't do a thing,' I retorted defensively, showing my hands in case Maya thought I'd pinched him.

'No, the animal is *un monstre*. He's bitten me, *mon derrière, c'est dégueulasse*. He should be shot.'

'At least it wasn't your face.' He gave me an unimpressed look. Well I could hardly offer to kiss his *derrière* better. I knew I wasn't very sympathetic, but it's strange how ugly boys can look when they pull faces at you.

'Oh, poor François, where does it hurt? Shall I kiss it better?' Maya was suddenly offering, cooing over him.

'I wouldn't if I were you, Maya. There's still spit on his bum, where the camel tried to kiss him. You never know what diseases they carry.'

Antony, Hercules, Everyone . . .

'Everybody's been here – loads of pirates and probably even Hercules. Can't you just feel the history?' I said dramatically. 'It's amazing when you think I might be standing exactly where, well, Antony stood.'

'Who?'

'Antony, as in *Antony and Cleopatra*? Shakespeare?'

'Whatever. I wanna go in the caves, Dad,' demanded Maya. 'Let's go down.' She turned to François.

'Anyone else for the caves? Lily, François?' Brett asked. 'Group vote.'

'No, not really, but you go ahead,' I said. 'I'll stay here and look at the sea. Or I'll sit on the beach. Honest. Go. I won't move. I promise not to get lost.'

I am not crazy about dark, damp, caves full of stalagmites and stalactites – things to trip over or bump your head on. I don't like the animals that like caves much either, but I could understand why Maya might. There was something gothic about Maya that had been hiding ever since François appeared; maybe a cave might remind her of her natural state. She wasn't even wearing her hair in plaits any more.

'We're not leaving you alone, not after yesterday. You're coming too,' said Maya's dad.

Ancient History

If it hadn't been for Maya's dad's appetite, we might still be stuck in the spooky, wet, dark caves. The only one who really seemed to enjoy them was Maya. Brett finally demanded that we find a restaurant. The waiter/owner of the restaurant we found asked if we were on our way to Lixus, to the Gardens of the Hesperides, where Hercules went in search of the golden apples. I think

113

we'd all had enough of Greek mythology by then, except Olivier. 'It's also to do with Paris and Helen of Troy, *oui*? It's where the tree with the golden apples grew, and the Goddess of Discord chose the Apple of Contention, that Paris would reward Aphrodite with. Paris was a simple goatherd,' Olivier explained to us, just in case we'd confused him with the capital of France. 'Three Greek goddesses came down to earth and asked Paris to choose which was the most beautiful of them. He chose Aphrodite and gave her the golden apple that he had been given. She in return gave him the most beautiful mortal woman on earth, Helen of Troy. Unfortunately Helen was already married to another man.' He looked peculiarly towards Nancy, who laughed. 'And so, the battle of Troy began, to get her back, and it went on for years. Now they think the Golden Apple was more likely to have been a tangerine.'

It was beginning to be a bit like a fruity history lesson. Thank goodness for Olivier's gorgeous French accent. If only all teachers at school could speak with a sexy French accent, I'm sure we'd learn much more.

'Well I sure know who the most beautiful woman on earth is.' Brett smiled cheesily at his wife, in a way I had never ever seen my dad do to Mum. I wondered if he did it to Suzi. I guess old people being soppy is quite cute – if Maya hadn't been making vomiting noises. 'OK, OK,

114

shall we go, guys?' said Brett.

'I was kind of looking forward to a siesta,' Nancy replied.

'Mum! Don't be gross! And when are we going to get the rest of our costumes? And I've got a headache. I swear it's going to thunder.'

'*Quoi?*' I had to ask. Since when had Maya become a weather girl?

'I always get headaches when a storm's coming on,' she explained.

'Wow, you are a witch! Why not cast a spell for a costume?' François asked.

'Because, François, I'm more like an ancient Roman soothsayer – an oracle, if you will. Let me take you back down into the caves and I'll read your future in the pools which were once my home. Ah, already I see your future is with an American girl.'

'Is this like a joke? You are – 'ow you say – pushing my leg?' asked François, wide-eyed.

We looked at him and shook our heads. 'No it's all true and we're definitely not pushing your leg, ever,' I told him. We tried to keep from smiling. Sometimes he could look so wide-eyed and cute.

'Wow, *très* spooky!'

If only all boys were really so gullible they'd believe anything.

Back at Base Camp

We got back to the hotel and the heavens opened. Maya went to rest in the room. She had a migraine, and she needed 'absolute darkness and quiet'. I knew I should've been working out my costume, but somehow my heart wasn't in it, especially as I was banned from making any noise in the room.

I went to check my emails, as everyone went off in different directions. I took my bag of books and drawing stuff, as I definitely intended to start painting. It had been a nice day, without all the annoyances of the day before. Even François and Maya hadn't been that irritating. It was better since they'd stopped whispering and cooing, and I felt a lot less excluded.

So off I trotted, smiling on my way to the computer room. No one was there, so I sat down and logged in.

Mum had sent a fairly Mum-ish email as per any time I go away.

Subject: Re: Still Alive

Darling Lil,

Glad you're loving Tangier and the hotel. Sorry to hear Maya is lovesick!

Well done for writing to the two grans. Poppy has disappeared off with Nick to Cornwall. Haven't seen or heard from the pathetic (putrid, pallid, pecunious, pathogenic – could go on forever with the computer thesaurus) Pat since. You are herewith given my full and complete backing to be as charming to him at school as you can stand. There is nothing like putting people in a foul mood by being overly sweet and nice to them (you should try it!).

Talking of which, your father, the one with the black mark by his name for bad behaviour in the name of Satan, has a black eye to match. Apparently he fell over into the rubbish bin on the way home, so he said, though how can he remember? I wouldn't have blamed Suzi for punching him. Anyway, he is terribly contrite and full of apologies to the point where his cheque book came out. Poppy was very happy, but as I said, it doesn't excuse his behaviour, or make it more forgivable. We all got a little carried away.

Meanwhile, don't run away with Peter O'Toole or any other handsome devil in a kaftan and a moustache like Omar Sharif or Borat! Have a fantastic New Year's Eve, and I'll see you at the airport. Call me if there are any delays. Oh, and say thank you to Maya and her parents. Bay's missing you lots.

Kisses and hugs.

Mum X X

I didn't feel as good as I expected to feel about Mum and Mr Taylor, horrible as he was as a teacher. I wanted Mum to be happy and it wasn't fair that Dad should have Suzi and Mum had no one apart from us kids. She deserved more. I would have to put my mind to finding Mum the perfect boyfriend; she was obviously far too confused to do it herself. Perhaps I should post up her details on a website if I could find a nice photo of her. I mean, lots of men were looking for an arty, batty, wine-drinking, cigarette-smoking, mother of three, weren't they? Well, they would if they knew her like I do. Maya's mum might be glamorous but she wasn't all squidgy and Mum-ish.

Subject: Quick Note to Lily from Bea

You all right? You didn't sound your usual flipityjipityjolity self?

Am off to La Français in 15 mins.

Billy is still lovely and still tall.

Billy does not have a moustache.

I hear moustaches can be the home of mice, beetles, nesting creatures, etc.

Beware! Don't go near them.

Have as much fun as is possible in the kasbah with sheep eyeball stew. *Vive la France*, *Vive la* Lily LaLa. And I'll be seeing you lots next year. Doesn't that sound odd?

Buzzzzzzz B

I was just thinking that I knew Bea would understand and then make me laugh, when I felt someone standing behind me. At first I thought it must be a ghost, because I hadn't heard anyone come in. I was staring intently at the screen wondering if Moroccan ghosts were better or worse than British ones, and they understood English or if I would have to speak French, when I heard a spectacularly non-ghost-like laugh.

'Lily LALA, ha ha!'

I knew his charm was a passing phase.

'*Bonjour* François, *comment allez vous?*'

'I'm going nowhere, I'm here to see you, Lily LaLa.' And he started singing 'La la Lily Lily la la Lily Lily la la' to the tune of the cancan.

'That was for private consumption. Not for you to read!'

'I thought I might check my emails. I have friends too, you know.'

'You have friends? Well done! There's a computer. Nothing stopping you. *Rien!*'

'I thought you were my friend, that you were liking me, *non?* Why are you being so, so, not liking me?'

I was momentarily silenced by his directness – an unusual sensation for me. Why was I being 'so not liking him'? Because he was so liking Maya? What a prime rat that made me. Instead of saying a normal 'sorry' I heard myself dramatically saying, '*Je suis désolée, François. Pardon. Je suis pardon.*'

And what did he do? He burst out laughing and replied, 'Not only are you pretty, you are a comedienne actress as well? *Très bien, Lily, ma petite fleur.*'

'*Merci.*'

'*Pas de quoi.* Hey, how you would like to play *au ping pong*?'

'Sorry, I only play table tennis.'

'OK, we play table tennis. Hey, you are quite funny.'

'Really?' I teased.

'Yes, really, Lily.'

And without replying to either email, off I skipped, laughing with not a care in my little Lily head about the world, wars, global warming, or even Maya. My head had been turned by a few complimentary words.

Checkmate

After some pretty intense competitive jumping about, François suggested we got a drink.

'Just when it looks like I'm beating you, huh?' I said.

'*Mais non.* I am the champion.'

We laughed down the stairs and then sat and watched the rain that was still pouring down and played something that didn't involve me sweating, my bosoms jiggling up and down and my face going bright red – chess. We sat and talked for ages in front of the board. He told me all about his life. All about how his mum and dad were breaking up, and how his dad had asked him to be nice to Maya, so that he would have a more favourable chance of getting his next picture produced by Nancy. Why were grown-ups so awful, conniving and manipulative? I felt so sorry for him, but I felt sorrier for Maya. I really did.

To try and make him feel better I told him about how awful it was when my mum and dad got divorced – all the screaming and shouting and slamming of doors that seemed to be part of every row. I thought about telling him about Christmas, but since I'd sworn to forget it, I didn't. He told me he'd liked me from the moment he saw me on the plane. I knew it had been true, that I hadn't been making it up, just by the way he'd looked at me, his eyes, the way we talked. Sometimes it's possible to really connect, even with a boy. Eyes can't lie, can they?

At least it proved that I wasn't going mad, but I couldn't carry on looking into his toffee-swirl eyes and listening to his gorgeous voice. I'd start to really like him – and then what about poor Maya? What were we going to tell her? That what she had with François was a sham and that this – François and I – was the real deal? Of course I couldn't. I wouldn't do anything to hurt her.

Room Service
Brett interrupted us. 'Hey guys, there you are! Playing

121

chess? Interesting. You must teach Maya sometime. By the way Maya's not up for dinner. She says she just wants quiet. We've already booked a place round the corner. We're going to head off in half an hour if you want to get ready. Now the rain's stopped, we're walking.'

I hadn't even noticed that the rain had stopped or that the sky was darkening or that I was losing. It felt like we'd only been sitting there for ten minutes.

'I should just stay with Maya,' I replied.

'I don't think she'd want that, honey,' said her dad with a kindly smile. 'She kinda likes being alone when she's not feeling too good.'

'I'll go and ask her. François and I could both stay with her.'

'We could order room service,' he suggested.

'What a great idea.' Already I was imagining a movie on the TV, ordering up some club sandwiches, French fries and lashings of lemonade, and topping it off with the blood-orange sorbets that I'd noticed on the menu. Maya would fall asleep early and I'd be left to talk to François. Hmm. Maybe it was better to be with the grown-ups after all – I couldn't trust myself to be alone with François, not the way he kept looking at me and touching my hand. Maya was ill upstairs and we were flirting and laughing downstairs. Just the sort of friend every girl needed – not! Anything between François and me would have to wait until he'd finished whatever he had with Maya.

As soon as I walked into our room, and as soon as I saw Maya, I knew room service was the last thing on her mind. She ran past me with all the speed of an Olympic athlete going for a world record in sick-hurling, into the loo.

'Just go, just go,' were her hurried instructions to my suggestion.

'Are you sure I can't get you anything?'

'Other than this?' She waved her hand over the various trays of food her mother had been bringing her all afternoon. 'Don't worry, I've taken my medicine. Have fun. I just need sleep. No more trays, or my mum barging in every ten minutes. Keep her out for as long as possible.'

'If you're sure, Maya.'

'I'll call her on my cell phone if there's an emergency. OK?'

'OK.' I dressed in double-quick time, brushed my hair in two strokes, lip-gloss-smudged my lips, then I was out of the door.

'*Oh là là, tu es parfaite.*' I felt myself blushing under François's gaze. Was this the same boy from this morning who'd made faces at me, and was I the same girl? And if I was this excited tonight, what was it going to be like at the party tomorrow – and would Maya be well enough to go? Part of me wanted her not to be, and I knew I was evil for thinking that.

'*Merci monsieur,*' I replied, and tried not to look at him.

I'm not sure why, but whenever I spoke French, it made François laugh.

On Parade

It was a strange dinner. Lovely, but definitely strange. We walked down from the hotel, away from the kasbah and the mysterious medina down the Rue de la Liberté, across the Place de la France, with its stalls of women selling the rough weave blankets they wear as skirts and we use as rugs. The coffee bars were thrumming with people sitting and watching the world walk by in the soft blue dusk. Arabic was blaring from the cafés' radios and televisions.

As we reached the restaurant, somebody or something let out a huge stream of expletives – words that even Granny 1 didn't use (and that's saying something). We all looked at each other in disbelief. Maya's parents discussed going elsewhere, until I looked round the door and saw the culprit: a white-and-grey parakeet in a large Victorian cage sat on the end of the bar shouting swearwords. The other people sitting around the old Thirties' bar were definitely odd, and some exceedingly old. The barman couldn't have been less than eighty years old himself. It was like being in a movie from at least fifty years ago, but everyone had aged in it.

François and I had non-alcoholic cocktails at the bar, poured over smashed ice. I could get used to cocktails! Then we sat down to dinner in a conservatory full of beautiful flowers and looked at the menu, which was completely English. Not English-nowadays food but old-fashioned English: Brown Windsor soup, potted shrimps, cottage pie, steak and kidney pudding, roast pheasant and partridge, treacle tart, lemon syllabub, Eton Mess. I'd seen recipes for this kind of food in Granny 2's old cookbooks, but I'd never seen anything like it in a restaurant. I don't think the grown-ups had either, as they kept asking what each thing was. Still, as Granny 1 would say, 'Give me an experience any day!'

It must have been the strangeness of the place, but I swear when Brett went to the bathroom, I saw Olivier put his hand on Nancy's leg in a distinctly over-friendly way. She smiled woodenly and sharply smacked back his hand as if it were a large mosquito, before whispering something back to him that turned him a little pale. I pretended that nothing had happened.

It was hard to believe that someone who spoke so beautifully could be such a rotter! As if getting his own son to suck up to the producer's daughter wasn't bad enough, as well as embarrassing him by saying he didn't read when he spoke another language fluently and could recite poetry. He was obviously a cad of the lowest sort. No wonder his wife was divorcing him! I thought my father was bad. Oh, poor François!

CHAPTER SEVEN

The End of the Year, World, Universe

31st December — All Advice Gratefully Considered

Subject: Trouble

Dear Bea,

I know you are in France and won't read this till for ever, but I will burst if I don't tell someone. I can't tell Maya for obvious reasons. I think I may have, sort of, kind of fallen for the Frenchie, François. There, said it. So *un petit problème*, as so has Maya.

I know he fancies me, too. You can just tell, can't you? It's the way someone looks into your eyes and pretends to read your palm, just so they can hold your hand. Anyway it's doomed. I am doomed.

I can't tell Maya any of this, or how François shared his ice cream with me, or other such delicious details.

Why is love so cruel, especially on New Year's Eve when it should be the beginning of a brand spanking New Year of happiness? On the good side, we went swimming together and the sun shone and I thought about you shivering away in Wet and Windy Ol' France. But I suppose you won't be shivering if you're all covered by Billy's arms and kisses . . . Don't make me as sick as a Tangier donkey!

Fancy-dress party tonight. Excitingly frightening! Arghh! And I'm a pirate. Maybe I can hold François hostage, ha ha me hearties. I shall steal the treasure. If only I could bring him back home.

Happy NYE

Your Lily-livered black-hearted best mate XX

I couldn't write to Mum. I couldn't write to anyone without putting down my conundrum, and I didn't want to worry her. I could write to Granny 1. Granny 1 never minded being worried. I think it's because she's so old and every agony seems a trifle after eighty years. But I opened up my diary instead.

Back to the Diary Room

Dear Diary,

I have been dressed and ready for ages. I am sitting on the balcony overlooking the pool, listening to the birds chirping along to the distant wailing from the mosque. What a racket!

I love François! There – I have said it. I love François. ♥ ♥ *François* ♥ ♥ *François x. François xxxxxx. He is as dreamy as a dream, so perfect that if he were a sweet he would be butterscotch-flavoured, all the way through, yummy. Delectable, deliriously délicieux.*

We spent all morning together. He was teaching me rude French words and I was melting into his chocolate-button-brown eyes. They are like toffee éclairs with chocolate in the middle. They also remind me of the chocolate fountain Mum took me to see at the Serpentine Gallery once in Kensington Gardens. It smelled delicious, but when I dipped my finger in, it tasted disgusting. Then I saw the sign that said, This Is Not Real Chocolate. *What a cheat! I don't suppose his eyeballs would taste of chocolate either. There is much that is unfair in life. François and me – the love that cannot be allowed. I wonder what he's been doing all afternoon? Thinking of me? I can't think of anything else. I don't care about my costume or the rest of my life and definitely not school. If I had only one question to ask God it would be: why is life SO CRUEL???*

I'll probably never be able to eat again. I shall waste away until they do my autopsy and find the reason for death is an extreme fracturing of the heart. Unmendable, even with the latest technology. François could fix it with a look or a word.

How can I be expected to think about fun at a time like this? Except I shall see him again soon. What do I look like? I can't get to the make-up mirror as Maya is still in the bathroom. She's feeling better, soaking in a tub and applying ten tons of make-up to her face before putting on all the stuff she's bought. Amazing how quickly she felt better, once she heard François and me speaking French together. Can I help it that we have so much in common – like the whole of Paris, France, and the poetry of our futures melding together like couplets?

What Are You Supposed to Be?

'Are you ready? Da da! Waddya think? Pretty cool, huh? I'll be the belle of the ball, dontchya think?' Maya twirled around the room like a Disney toy.

'What are you supposed to be, exactly? I thought we were both going as pirates?'

'No. I wanted to be original, so I'm a princess of the dunes, of course. Duh!'

'Of course, I've known so many. Is that a knife?' I was so irritated that I suddenly didn't want to go to the party. She had double-crossed me.

'It's a real silver dagger.'

'You'd be arrested for knife crimes in London.'

'We're in Morocco. Hey, you haven't seen the *pièce de résistance* – it's a real Moroccan headpiece made of silver and turquoise. Do you like it? Mum got it for me. I swear it made my headache vanish.'

'Since when did you start speaking French?' I asked, trying to ignore the magic healing jewelled crown that turned her into a queen amongst princesses. I was seriously depressed. I looked as authentically pirate as Bay looked like a Viking or a cowboy; in fact he'd win the competition. I had an embroidered waistcoat over my white ruffled shirt and a scarf tied around my head. My trousers were tucked into my pirate boots and with my earrings I'd thought I'd look OK. But Maya looked just gorgeous.

'*Pièce de résistance*? That's American. And when did you start getting so crabby?'

'I'm not crabby, I just . . . Oh, I just hate my costume. Maybe I should wear my orange ball gown after all and go as a Fifties' prom girl.'

'Maybe you'd look more the part if you used my eye make-up and this chunky silver belt of mine. And where's your eye-patch?'

'I've just finished making one and its total crappydom.'

Un-wowed by Me

I knew she was trying to help, but all I could think of was

how François would be wowed by her, and deeply un-wowed by me. Maya had the X-factor wrapped into every bit of her belly dancer's outfit. Her body had escaped for the night from under her usual shield of black clothes and she had a perfect-shaped tummy for it. How is life even remotely fair? I tied my patch round my head and hoped I wouldn't bump into too many things.

'Hey, you look great, you could be in *Pirates of the Caribbean*,' Maya said.

'Great! As long as I don't look like Johnny Depp. Actually, lend me that black eyebrow pencil.' I drew a huge dastardly moustache across my upper lip and adjusted my ruffled shirt. I might not have the flesh of a belly dancer on show, but I looked good enough to be funny.

'Cool. If you're ready we should go down to meet them in the bar . . .'

Just then there was a knock at the door. 'That'll be Mum.'

As I was closer, I opened the door. '*Mais non, ce n'est pas possible, tu es trop ravissante*, too beautiful.' François was at the door. I however, was behind it, hiding as he professed his adoration. '*Magnifique*, Maya. You look too beautiful.'

'Yes, doesn't she just?' I jumped out from behind the door.

'Oh Lily, you are a very funny pirate. You both look

great.' My heart plummeted into my uncut-toenail dirt, and then zoomed up like a rocket, blocking my throat with its detritus. I swallowed hard and tried to keep all emotion out of my voice. Damn! I should have worn that orange Fifties' dress, but Maya had advised me that the pirate outfit was more appropriate; I started to think I might know why.

'And what are you meant to be, exactly?' I asked François.

François was wearing a strange cap, shirt, baggy shorts and medals. 'I'm a French Foreign Legionnaire.'

'Legionnaires? Hey, isn't that a disease?' I wittily replied. No one laughed but me.

'Hey, your parents say we must go *vite*! The taxi is already here for us.'

There was no time to change. I would have to go as the comedy pirate.

The Garden of Eden

We had driven up into the hills above the city. The taxi stopped by a huge gate in the middle of a large wall that seemed to be encompassing an entire compound. Below us shone Tangier's twinkling lights and the bobbing boats in the harbour.

'I think we're going to one of those gated communities,' I said to Maya, but she gave me a 'So what?

Who cares!' look. I continued. 'You know, like the ones near you that they built to keep the very rich weird people away from us normal people.'

'They did not. It's for security, isn't it, Dad?'

'What's that, honey?'

But it was soon clear to me as we arrived that this wasn't a gated community. 'It's one great big mansion.'

'I bet it's bigger than Blake's house. Lily's boyfriend, Blake, lives in an English mansion. Isn't that right, Lily?' said Maya, helpfully explaining to François. Thereby François thought that I had a boyfriend, and a rich one. Normally I wouldn't mind, except I saw François's eyes look all disappointed at me as if I was the blaggard, just because I was dressed as a pirate!

'Is this true, Lily?'

'No, he's my ex, and this is about a quarter the size. It's not nearly as grand or as old as Blake's house in England,' I told François. 'Still this is large enough. I wouldn't want to have to clean it.' Then I saw the garden and added, 'Let alone do the gardening.'

'Duh. I think they have servants for that,' Maya informed me.

The garden was huge and hung with glowing Chinese lanterns. There was a band playing the kind of music you can dance to, but you wouldn't want to. It was kind of swinging old people's music that mums and dads like.

Everybody was in wonderful fancy dress – ornate costumes *à la* Marie Antoinette and Louis XVI swished past us in the hallway. I tried to stop thinking about how rubbish I looked, and how François kept looking at Maya. One woman had a lamb on a ribbon. I thought if she wasn't ninety she might have been trying to be Little Bo Peep. I supposed Little Bo Peep had to get old too. I was quite consciously gawping. I knew it was rude but I couldn't help it. Even the people serving drinks and food on silver platters were dressed in eighteenth-century wigs and outfits. They looked like they'd stepped out of the paintings that lined the walls. The place was amazing, with old paintings and furniture everywhere, not just Moroccan stuff. It made even Maya's costume look ordinary.

'Wow, Olivier, thanks so much for bringing us to this great party,' I heard Brett say.

'You are such a sweetie,' added Nancy, kissing him firmly on the cheek. Even though she was dressed like Cleopatra, she was behaving thoroughly like the good wife, arms linked with her husband's. I wondered, after the other night's hand slap, if she was trying to tell Olivier something?

Infested by Pirates

We were introduced to about a hundred people within

the first half hour. Many were on holiday and we recognised a few from our hotel. Some were English, and there were a couple of Americans, but most were Spanish or French. Though some were interesting, I was relieved when François tapped me on the shoulder and motioned to me to follow him. He got me into a corner and asked urgently, 'You do believe me that it's you I adore, Lily? You are the most beautiful girl here.'

The way he looked at me, I could only nod. Then he leaned into me and kissed me. It was all so perfect I could have fainted, but we managed to tear ourselves apart when we saw Maya come out of the loo. 'I didn't know you were waiting,' she said, and dragged François off while I pretended to go to the loo.

Usually there's nothing I love more than investigating new loos in hotels or other people's homes. Often they are the most fascinating and revealing room in a house: what handwash, towels, books, magazines, pictures on the walls, etc. do they have? But I couldn't take any of it in. I stood in front of the mirror in there and thought, Lily, this is another fine mess you got me into. What do I do next?

I raced after them, to see Maya dragging François off to the garden. Obviously I had to follow. I needed to know what they were getting up to. I would have to tell her at some point that it was me he adored. Maybe he was taking her outside to tell her the truth. I watched them out of the corner of my eye (the one not covered by my pirate patch). Someone then started asking me about my costume, diverting my attention.

'So did you know Tangier was infested by pirates after the fourteenth century? It became a lawless state until the Portuguese stepped in, and after that the English took over.'

'Really? How very, deeply, fascinating.' I smiled back, desperate to escape. Why do adults always feel they need to tell you things just when you're involved in really important life-and-death stuff? When I finally managed to escape, I turned around to look for Maya and François, and found they'd disappeared. I was searching in the lantern light around the garden but it was too vast and shadowy to see them, and there were too many people milling around – they could have gone anywhere.

Just when I was about to give up I thought I saw the back of François's khaki outfit sneaking behind a huge gardenia bush. I tiptoed up behind it, then climbed in closer. There was some hideous giggling, and I tried to listen for any misplaced words of passion. Obviously it was him – I recognised his gorgeous voice – but what was he doing with Maya when he'd just kissed me? His father was probably putting pressure on. Obviously Maya looked brilliant, obviously I was green as a grasshopper,

137

but I was the only girl there with a moustache. That must count for something, surely?

'Oh Franswaar, I'm so glad we got some time to be alone. I'm glad you managed to escape that awful girl,' I heard her say.

How could Maya be talking such mushy rubbish? The poor deluded fool actually believed that he wanted to be with her? Who was she kidding? And how dare she be so rude about me – I wasn't that awful!

But I wasn't prepared for his reply.

'I am so desolate when I am away, but you know you are the most beautiful girl here – in the world. I cannot stay away from you.'

She giggled revoltingly, and there were definite sounds of snogging – unless it was just two halves of a watermelon being squashed together.

I was outraged – hideously horrified. Was he really that good an actor?

Then she said, 'What's desolate mean, Franswaar?'

I was almost vomiting in the bushes, at just how mushy and dumb Maya sounded – it didn't sound like her at all. Since when had she forgotten the contents of her dictionary? 'What's desolate?' Indeed! Could this really be my smart friend? How could I get her away when she had all the traits of a magnetic limpet, and that was just in her voice? I hated to think where her arms were –

probably draped around his neck like a scarf or a boa constrictor.

I decided I had to act, but disentangling myself from the bushes without causing a scene was easier said than done, especially with only one eye in use. Eventually I squeezed out on my belly, adjusted my eye-patch and climbed a nearby tree to see what was actually going on. I scratched my body on another tree, before clambering on to a branch. When I looked down, I saw François's head glued to a girl's face. Unfortunately her face was obscured, but one thing I could clearly make out was that this girl had blond hair, not black like Maya's. So:

1) the lighting was very odd,
2) I was hallucinating or mad, or else
3) it wasn't Maya at all.

On balance, number three seemed the most likely. François was whispering his words of love to some blonde floosie he picked up like a germ from God knows where! Yuck!

Where was Maya? What was I to do?

Breaking it Gently

I had to find Maya – this was too much information to contain alone. Besides, I thought she might be a tiny bit interested in what François was doing in his spare time. I raced around through the garden and through the house. Finally I found her in a drawing room.

'There you are, Maya, I've been looking for you everywhere. Have you seen François?' I asked her, not knowing quite how to break things gently to her.

'Lily, there you are. No, not for ages. He just disappeared on me. He said he was going to the loo and never reappeared. Do you think he's all right? I mean he might have a stomach bug. I don't want to disturb —'

'I think he needs disturbing, quite badly.' I pulled her outside, pointed behind the bushes and put my finger to my lips.

'What do you mean?'

We pulled back the bushes together and then all four of us shrieked!

NYE Flood Warnings

Maya turned and ran, and I chased after her as her sobs filled the night air. Heads turned as she fled through the crowds of people.

Of course I felt sorry for her, but what about me? All his sweet talk obviously meant nothing – he was a 'scoundrel and a blaggard', as they say in old pirate slang. I thought of all he had said, all he had whispered to me only hours before in the hotel corridor: 'I like your funny moustache, it is *très* – 'ow you say – sexy?' If he hadn't been looking at me with those chocolate-button eyes of

140

his, and speaking with that gorgeous Parisian voice, and kissing my fingers and mouth, obviously I would have laughed out loud at him. 'My moustache was 'ow you say sexy! Honestly, François!' I'd have said, but as I thought about it, my stomach caved in and did a little trampoline double back-flip. I know technically this isn't possible, but just wait until it happens to you; it's as if there's a trapeze artist juggling inside your body.

Now I knew it definitely wasn't me he loved, or Maya either, and it probably wasn't even The Blonde.

Why was my life so full of drama all the time?

But suddenly, as Maya collapsed into a hurricane of tears on the grass, François seemed less important. I offered a few platitudes and slowly the sniffles began to dry up. Eventually she said, 'I don't know whether to like you or hate you, Lily. You know the US cavalry used to chop the heads off the messengers when they arrived with bad news.'

'Look, it's going to be midnight soon,' I said, trying to cheer her up. 'Shall we try and find your mum and dad? Speak of the devil – I mean, there are your parents.'

Maya's parents appeared in time to give us a glass of champagne and sing 'Auld Lang Syne'. We all crossed hands and sang about friendship, and then we hugged. As Maya was busy hugging her parents, I wondered if Mum, Bay and Poppy, or Dad and Suzi, were thinking about me and wishing I was with them, as much as I wished I was. I felt all weepy.

Later That Night

That night I managed to write only a few words in my (technically out-of-date) diary, before collapsing asleep with my head in its pages.

> *Dear Diary*
> *Happy Happy New Year! Maybe I am getting older or madder, but that definitely wasn't my idea of how to spend New Year's Eve! I know now I'm fourteen that I'm a lot more mature in my approach to life, boys, friendship, the universe – that must be it. But it doesn't explain why I had to have such a crazy New Year's Eve. Zzzzz.*

What on earth was I trying to say? I know neither of us brushed our teeth that night, or turned out the light, but we must have both wished that the New Year would only get better. But would it?

CHAPTER EIGHT
Love All

1st January – Resolutions, Resolutions, Resolutions

'Have you made any New Year resolutions?' I asked Maya in my most chatty, friendly Lily voice, trying to break the ice. We were both still lying in bed, pretending to be asleep. I knew she was awake, but she wasn't talking to me.

I knew that I had thought François loved me, and obviously Maya had thought that he'd loved her. Only François and I knew the real truth of his father's and his skulduggery! Should I really shatter her illusions? *Mon Dieu!* Should I tell her that François was only interested in her so that his dad could work on a movie with her mum? Would it be more mature to keep that information to myself? Possibly – but would I be able to?

I knew what my resolutions were going to be for the coming year. I'd been writing them down in my diary since I woke up.

1) Never have the same taste in boys as your mates – très dangereux!

2) Find an anger management therapist for my parents and Poppy before next Christmas. (Or it might be easier to swap them on eBay.)

3) Change schools (or get Mr Taylor sent on a long, slow, dark voyage to Outer Mongolia).

4) Start writing poetry so I can escape to another life and be a famous poet in Paris.

5) Practise French so much that it stops sounding sexy with its oo-la-la-ness. (Except when I want it to.)

'No. What's the point in resolutions? No one ever keeps promises,' Maya grumpily replied from under her covers. Then when her head popped out, she gave me a weird look. She was still mad at me for bursting her bubble I guess – for being the messenger. Meanwhile, I was getting mildly irritated by her tone. Neither of us knew how to talk about last night. A knock at the door brought relief.

'Ah, that sounds like *nos petits-déjeuners.*'

'No I assure you, Lily, it's our breakfast. But at least a

croissant might keep you quiet.'

'What do you mean?' I faked astonishment that Maya wouldn't want to listen to me talking, given the chance.

'Because I want you to shut up so I can think about last night – all the things François said to me in that jasmine-scented garden. I know he's in love with me. I know the other girl meant nothing to him. He said so; they weren't even kissing.'

There – she had broken our silent taboo and spoken directly about HIM; used the François name in its full vanity.

'I'm sure she didn't mean anything to him,' I replied. I knew where François's affections lay – with himself. And they were jolly well kissing when I saw them.

Rude Food

Once again for breakfast we feasted like kings, as we had done every day since we'd got to Tangier. Sometimes it was a relief not to be pushing more food down my gullet. The problem was it all just tasted so good, and how could I turn down a delicious meal when I knew what awaited me back at home in my own dear mother's kitchen/fridge/oven? I know she tries, but Mum's cooking is an insult to food – a choice of off-offerings (sometimes I swear you can hear dead tomatoes, blue with cold and green with mould, pleading to be let out so they can escape the fridge to a decent burial in a compost heap) or burned offerings (as in this-sausage-has-already-met-its-maker-several-times-and-the-last-was-an-Aztec-sun-god).

'You finished stuffing your face?' Maya interrupted her beauty regime in front of the mirror to ask me.

'Have you finished plastering yours?' I replied.

'Why are you so bugged? Because I still have a boyfriend, and you haven't managed to split us up?'

'I wasn't trying to split you up. I thought you'd want to know who his other friends were. Next time I'll keep my mouth shut. Strange – I didn't hear your reconciliation on the way home. Or did I miss something?'

'It's none of your business. François loves me. It's a reality. The truth!'

'Whose truth, Maya? I'd tell you the truth, but I don't think you want to hear it.'

At which point she stomped off to the shower.

The Definition of Love

While we dressed, I thought it was time to try to talk to Maya properly. I don't know what made me more uncomfortable – angry depressed silences, or blazing shouting rows. Maya didn't seem overly keen, but I felt I had to tell her the truth.

'Look, Maya, you know how much I value our

146

friendship, but I feel I have to be straight about this whole François thing. I told you on the plane about fancying a boy. Well, it was François, and when you were ill he led me to believe, well, that he liked me, a lot.' I could see Maya's face growing red with fury. 'I promise, at no time did I ever flirt with him. I wouldn't do anything like that. I'm your friend first.' I crossed my fingers behind my back remembering our furtive kiss the night before.

'So why didn't you make it clear before?' she replied.

'Well, because you suddenly seemed so struck by him. You changed. I thought I couldn't really say anything – not after you'd invited me away on this holiday and your parents were paying for everything. It would've been rude.'

'And it's not rude now? Anyway, they haven't paid for everything. Mum got the money off your dad.'

'Oh!' I was literally struck dumb. For once, I didn't know what to say. Not only had my father paid for me to go away and have a wonderful holiday without him, when all I ever did was complain about him – but he hadn't even told me he had paid. I would try to be a nicer daughter in future (and I wouldn't swap him on eBay).

'So if you've got nothing else, and nothing ACTUALLY happened between you two, I'm going to find François and ask him to explain what was going on with the girl.

I'm sure it was completely innocent. I mean what if it turned out they're just cousins?'

Kissing cousins – I don't think so. What a revolting thought. I'd certainly never get that close to any of my cousins. 'Hmm, yes. Perhaps they're even brother and sister. There must be an ordinary explanation.'

I could see Maya in the mirror. I knew that even she wasn't totally convinced by the way she was biting her bottom lip. She always did that when she was nervous or indecisive.

The sounds of total hilarity and deafening splashes came through the open balcony window, and were getting louder.

'Oh Maya,' I said. 'It's too hot to argue, let's go and have a swim.'

'With all that noise down there? I wonder if there'll be room for us.'

'I hope it's not your parents starting a fight? Parents these days! What are they like?'

'What, like a pool fight?' Maya seemed to be mellowing. 'The first rule of fighting is: not in a pool!' She held her little fists up, boxing the air and ducking and diving her way to the window. Maya was funny.

I wondered why grown-up arguments always dwarfed whatever anyone else had going on. Was it just because they were louder or because there were more serious consequences to adult rows, like divorce? I sort of knew that whatever was happening with Maya, in the end we would make it up. Well I hoped we would eventually. François had kidnapped my heart, but he'd held Maya's ransom. I wondered if we would ever completely understand what had happened, or why.

'No, it's not them, but, oh Lily, look who it is.'

Betrayed

I looked over the balcony and I stared straight into the pool. François was in the pool with The Blonde! And the blonde girl we'd seen him with only last night wasn't just in the pool with him – she was sitting on François's shoulders, as if modelling for the illustration with a cross through it in my local swimming baths that clearly states *NO HORSEPLAY ALLOWED*. If that wasn't horseplay, I didn't know what was, and I thought we were in a Muslim country with higher morals than Chelsea and Kensington swimming baths! I was just about to shout down, 'What on earth do you think you're doing, *vous cochons?*' when Maya grabbed me and pulled me back into the room and behind the curtains.

'Shhh, Lily. Stop. Look, I've just thought of a plan. We'll get our own back on that little double-crossing French waiter. How dare he play us off against each other and then go off with some blonde bimbo!' Finally she was outraged. Maya had well and truly returned from outer space – I could see it in her eyes. 'I see he's just a cheap gigolo. Think he can mess us about, huh?'

'I'm so sorry, Maya, but you know what I said – there's worse. He's worse!'

'What? Out with it, Lily. I want every nasty piece of dirt, and then I'm going to rub his face in it.'

'Are you sure? I mean absolutely certain?' and she nodded her head decisively. Then I spilled out every one of François's cheap chat-up lies, and what he'd said about the thing with his dad. Well, I had truly lit the blue touchpaper. I waited for the explosion to happen, but it didn't. She just seemed resolute, her mouth fixed with a sturdy determination.

'I'm sorry too, Lily. He's so not worth it. Cheap and cheesy is too good a description for that weasel. Let's make a promise that we'll never let a boy get between us again.' We crossed our arms and slapped our palms.

'What's the plot then?' I asked.

'This is where François gets his . . . Oh baby, watch out!'

I've Put a Spell On You

'François?' I shouted, running out to the pool like a deranged idiot, in front of everyone. 'François, it's dreadful,' I said, ignoring the girl who had wound herself

150

around him like some Russian vine. 'Maya's discovered all about us!' I shouted out with all the melodrama of a prime-time soap.

Finally I 'saw' the girl. She was tiny, blonde of course, and very pretty. 'Hi,' I said. 'My name is Lily and I believe you know François?'

'Oh, are you the jealous ex-girlfriend he was trying to escape? He said you were a right American pain. You don't sound very American to me.'

'That's because I'm his girlfriend's best friend, and British. Perhaps you'd like to meet Maya? I know she'd love to meet you.'

Even the adults sat up and peered over their books.

I turned to François. 'Maya knows. She knows how much I truly love you, and how much you love me, and that we're going to run away together,' I shouted louder and more dramatically. 'Let's tell your father.'

'What are you talking about, Lily? Shhh! Shut up and be quiet, you silly little girl.'

'Quiet? Don't you want to tell the world about our secret love, my love?' I was giving it all I'd got, playing for the moment when Maya rushed out and sidled up to the pool. The Blonde, stunned and amazed by my obviously brilliant and convincing performance, and then faced with two distraught screaming girls, now backed away.

'How could you, François? How could you do this to me

– me?' Maya shrieked. 'I loved you – gave you everything I had and now this.' She pretended to break down into a waterfall of tears.

'You are crazee, *petites jeunes filles toquées!*'

'It's no good, François, you've been playing me for a patsy – I saw it all in my oracle. I told you I could read the future. I know what you've been up to, even before the blonde bint. I know that your father wanted you to make love to me, so that Mum would produce his film.'

An adult gasped at Maya's dirty revelations.

'Why you are saying these things?' François looked very worried indeed, scouting the balconies to see if the relevant adults had heard. He tried to slime back into her affections. '*Je t'adore, ma petite chérie.*' François looked like a trapped animal, his terrified eyes darting between me and Maya. The Blonde was now sitting on a sunbed behind him, clearly outraged as she practised some advanced pouting and snake hissing.

'You know that everything we've said is true, François. Don't think for a moment you can get around either of us,' I said.

'And don't think your cheesy French accent is going to help. I don't even know what you're saying. But now I've put a spell on you; from now on, no one is going to believe a word you say, especially not "I love you".'

'You are a witch? What spell, you mean *envoûter*? You

152

can't do this to me. Take it back.' We'd obviously hit a nerve – he was very highly superstitious.

'Sorry, François. You're going to have to be a lot nicer to us than that. We don't like your tone of voice. Oh sorry, you can't help it!' Maya laughed.

'And we're very busy and we'd like a swim, so can you just buzz off and get away from the pool? Now,' I told him.

'But —'

'Actually, we don't like anything about you, and if you want me to remove that spell . . .'

'I don't believe you. You are just a *bébé*, playing games.' He tried to bluff his disbelief, but once you realise that most human communication is done through reading someone's physical gestures, you can almost turn the volume off. He was scared.

'Oh really?' Maya stood there with her hands on her hips, commanding the situation with an evil smile playing around her mouth. Her eyes narrowed to cats' slits.

'I'm not sure getting on the wrong side of Maya is such a great idea, François. Really I'm not. You should see what she's done to boys in London.'

We managed to hold our faces straight until he'd gathered up his stuff and run back inside the hotel – but not before he suffered the final insult of The Blonde throwing a glass of orange juice into his furious face, before she stormed off.

It was all so hysterical, and emotions were running so high, that at one point I didn't know whether I was going to burst into tears or laughter. I'm glad we chose to laugh; it makes you feel so much better than crying.

Honestly, since when were boys ever worth coming between friends? I know I might think differently one day, but for the moment I was sticking with friends.

We dive-bombed into the pool together on the count of three, much to the annoyance of the other guests – but we had given them so much entertainment. Later, as we floated in the water I said, 'I'm sorry, it didn't work out for you and François. Especially since he was the first boy you liked. I'm sorry I was so stupid and jealous.' And I was, because I hadn't liked feeling like that.

'Yeah, well, I'm sorry I kept deserting you to spend time with that jerk. What can I say? Life sucks. Thank God there are compensations. Let's mend our broken hearts with some ice cream and hot chocolate sauce.'

'With extra strawberries?'

'And cream.'

So we did.

CHAPTER NINE
Oh, Sweet Pigeon Pie

2nd January – The Thing About Boys

'The thing about boys, girls, is that they will try to be in charge, but as soon as you challenge them, they know you mean business.'

We were walking around the grassy graveyard of St Andrews, the Anglican church up the road from the hotel. Apart from a few Moorish features (that's what the guidebook called a Sufi translation of the Lord's Prayer inscribed around the arch inside the church), you could have been anywhere in Britain: the church was surrounded by a stone wall, and you went through a little wooden gate and up a cobbled pathway to the church. Around the back, the graveyard was full of monuments to all the British, European and Americans who loved

Tangerines (or Tangier) so much that they lived and eventually died there.

I was thinking how strange it would be to live in another country where nothing was familiar. I suppose you must get used to it. I'd have to get used to living in Paris when I eventually moved there. I wandered along, engrossed in reading the dates and inscriptions on the gravestones; my imagination went off on a tangent as I thought about what their lives were like, and what mine was going to be like.

I had stopped by a tomb that was practically as big as some people's houses – it seemed a shame that only skeletons occupied it – when from the other side, I heard Maya's mum talking to Maya.

'What I mean is, François is just a boy, and he wanted to feel powerful. I'm sure his feelings for you were real, sweetie, but he's a teenager and probably the thought of him being able to charm you, let alone blondie, was overwhelming. Whatever he said to Lily about needing to get in with you for his dad's sake, getting him a film deal – it's total crap, I want you to know that. Movies don't get made like that.'

I couldn't hear Maya's reply, but there was a murmuring then a pause. Her mother continued; she had a voice that carried and I couldn't help but listen.

'Oh, honey. You know I'd never do anything to make

you unhappy, whatever François told you. You know I love your dad and if I thought for a moment that something like making a film with Olivier would damage that, I wouldn't do it. OK?'

I Spy

I felt like a spy and a traitor now, ear-wigging. This *espionnage* (as they say in French) was becoming a rather bad habit of mine. I would like to have blamed it on Tangier's influence – the ghosts of all the expatriate spies in this city in the Forties and Fifties. (No wonder they call them spooks!)

I quietly crept away from their conversation. I realised that it must be strange for Maya and her mum to be away from their home country, America. A week away on holiday was fine, but living abroad for years would be very hard.

All of these thoughts made me feel guiltier for even thinking about taking from Maya the one boy she had the slightest liking towards – even if he had turned out to be an idiot. I had realised a lot on this holiday. I'd always thought Maya's parents were rich and glamorous, which they are, but it's only skin deep and they're definitely not perfect.

'I'm just popping back inside the church for a minute,' I called over to Maya and her mum.

'Don't worry, Lily, we'll be here,' Nancy said, glowing in her pink trousers and orange-and-red zebra shirt, as vibrant as a burning bush.

Inside, the church was cool and dark. A little shiver went through me as I sat down on one of the pews and began my little prayer:

'Dear God,

'Please let Maya forgive me for being such a mean old cow, over a boy of all things. I didn't mean to, and I suppose nothing really happened, though I did have feelings of euphoria when he kissed me, I am ashamed to say.

'Also, look after Mum, Poppy and Dad, and Bay because however annoying and disgusting he is, he can also be very sweet. That's Bay, not Dad. Or maybe both.

'Please help me to be a better daughter, sister and friend. Help me to be good and kind and funny because laughing is very important – it makes us all happier.

'Thank you very much for all the things I have and for all the people who love me. I know it doesn't seem it sometimes, but I am grateful.

'Oh, and thank you for listening.

'Over and out, Lily.

'And, in case you get confused at where on earth this message is coming from, I'm in Tangier, not the usual London. But of course you'd know that, being omniscient. Oh, and thank you for letting me see this beautiful place – that's Tangier, I mean.'

Free

It is amazing how doing such a simple thing can make you feel an awful lot better. I don't know why everybody doesn't pray; it's free, it doesn't need any intelligence or knowledge and it doesn't make you fat or sick, like chocolate.

I practically skipped back outside and, unlike coming out of a church in Britain, the sky was clear and blue! Tomorrow I was going back home, where it would probably be freezing and wet, but Mum would give us crumpets with butter and thick English honey for tea, because she knows I like them (even if she burns them). Don't tell me there isn't a God; I just wish he'd taught her how to cook better!

'Over here, Lily,' said Maya, waving. Whatever Maya's mum had said to her had obviously done her some good because she was almost smiling.

'You both good to go?' her mum asked, walking towards me. 'Anything else you want to do on your last day? Lunch at the yacht club on the beach? Or buying gifts in the medina? You got your mum and dad something, right?'

'I thought I'd buy some stuff later on – get Dad some spices, and some kohl eye make-up and henna for Mum and Poppy, or maybe the other way round. There's nothing really to get for Bay.'

'Let's go there now. We might as well, before they close for lunch. We could get your brother a cute little Moroccan outfit. They're so sweet in miniature. And what about stopping at the perfume shop? It's world-famous. Does your Mum like perfume?'

'Is the Pope Catholic?'

'I guess so.'

Maya had told me about her mum's obsession with shopping, and within the hour we were suddenly laden down with bags and offers of visiting all the shopkeepers' homes for lunch – examples of the famous Moroccan hospitality.

'Mum, can we stop the shopping? We've really got to get back and reclaim the pool from François. We told him he wasn't allowed to be there without our permission.'

'I know, I'm not deaf. I think the whole hotel knows. We heard it all from the balcony yesterday. You jinxed his powers and hexed him back. Since when have you been *Bewitched*'s Tabitha?'

'Oh there's a lot of things you don't know about me, mother,' she said, straight as a Jane Austen character.

'Really? All I know is that you frightened the boy half dead.'

'Well it serves him right. He put a spell on us first,' said Maya.

'So we just put it back on him – simple really,' I said.

'You mean, "All is fair in love and war"?'

'Yes, except nothing's fair in war. We've plans for François,' Maya murmured.

'That poor boy! You two together make a considerable enemy.'

We were walking back down into the market where we had first gone. 'Oh Lily, don't you think that gold-and-blue jellaba would look absolutely adorable on your little brother with his blond hair? Let me buy it for him, I insist – he has to have it. He will look like such a doll with his bangs. And what about a brown one too? He'll look like a Jedi knight.' Maya and I looked at each other and laughed.

'What, like in *Star Wars*? Thank you. It'll go perfectly with his sword collection.'

'And boy, does he know how to use it!' Maya prodded her mum, and for a moment I missed that mischievous squadgeball.

Poolside

Maya and I decided to spend the rest of the day laid out on our sun beds, sharing Maya's MP3 player and clicking our fingers for François when we required drinks, snacks, or games bringing for our amusement. This was the life of luxury. But the final cherry on the top was when François finally broke down and apologised to Maya. I was in the loo when he said it was only her he loved, and begged her to stay in touch. Maya had predicted as much. And then, when she went to our room, he did the same to me, just as Maya told me he would. I swear there's something psychic about that girl. I gave him Maya's email address (Wednesdaygirl) and she gave him mine (Ukpowerflower). If he got in touch with either of us again we would know.

'Are all the boys in Paris as lovely and sincere and as romantic as you are, François?' I asked him, before he disappeared, to bolster his bruised ego by chatting up another hundred girls around Tangier's hotels.

'For Parisians, it comes naturally. We adore women, Lily, *fleur délicate, tu fais battre mon coeur . . .*'

His answer made me think seriously about my future plans of going to live in Paris. I wouldn't be able to survive a week if my heart was being torn up every half an hour by such handsome chocolate-brown-eyed rats, spouting romantic poetry that I couldn't understand.

The Last Mint Tea

'Do you realise this is our last mint tea?' I said wistfully to Maya. 'And our very last Moroccan pastry. And that was probably our last swim. Boo hoo.'

We were sitting up at the beautiful bar, warming ourselves with tea and nibbling greedily at the delicious pastries, whilst trying to stop them crumbling over the backgammon board. It reminded me of sitting there alone when Maya had been off smooching with François; funny, it seemed a million years ago. It also reminded me how embarrassed I was going to be when I next saw Bea after asking for her advice for the lovelorn! Eek! When you're in the middle of emotional entanglement, you can't see anything else, and then afterwards you can stand back and think, what was that about? Was I completely crazy? And the answer is often yes.

'It might have been yours, but I'm getting up early and going for a pre-breakfast swim,' Maya replied. 'Hey, let's do everything different tomorrow morning. We could have breakfast downstairs in the restaurant – have sweet pigeon-pie pastries?'

'Wow, you know how to live, Maya, I'll give you that! Pigeon for breakfast in Trafalgar Square from now on?'

'Oh, shurrup. If we packed tonight we could still fit in a swim and stuff before we leave for the airport.'

'What time are you going back to London?' Muhammed, the barman, asked. 'I shall have to make you fresh tangerine juice. You can't leave Tangier before you drink its juice.'

'That sounds delicious, thank you. We leave at ten-thirty a.m.'

'How can we be going tomorrow? The holiday feels like it's only just started,' I moaned.

'That is what everyone says when they come to Morocco. One day you will return.'

'I hope so,' I said. But next time, it would be without the boy trouble.

The Last Night

The phone was ringing as we opened the door to our room. Maya rushed to pick it up. For an eighth of a second, a host of horrible thoughts crowded through my mind. After all, who would be calling our hotel room? Who would have the number? Had some terrible disaster befallen someone?

1) What if a painting had fallen on her head and Mum went into a coma and didn't wake up for sixteen years and couldn't recognise Bay at nineteen, let alone me, and I'd be thirty?! Argh.

2) Or had Poppy, not looking when she crossed the road, got mushed under a bus wearing dirty pants and it was on national news? How would I ever show my face in school?

3) Or worse, had Dad decided to adopt another child and cut me off without a penny because he knew I was

the sort of daughter to push him over a cliff edge in a wheelchair?

Amazing how fast thoughts can zoom in and out of the brain. I swear the imagination is faster than the fastest Ferrari.

As it turned out, it was Maya's dad saying they'd meet us downstairs because we were going to have a drink somewhere before our last dinner in the hotel.

'Mum says this is our chance to dress up real special.'

This was the opportunity I'd been waiting for. If the last night wasn't the time to wear a bright-orange silk Fifties' cocktail dress, goodness knows when was – it was hardly the outfit for a school dance!

'I wonder where we're going? I thought our hotel had the smartest bar in Tangier?' I asked.

'I don't know, but it sounds exciting.'

There was a lot of girlish giggling as we got ready. At one point I looked at Maya laughing at something especially silly, and was sorry that it hadn't been like this the whole time. It could've been, and yet we let our stupidity get in the way.

'What! Why are you staring at me, freak?' I asked.

'Why would I want to stare at a chimpanzee, unless I wanted to see it pick its nose?'

'Yadda, yadda.'

'No really, Maya, I was just thinking what a waste. We

could have been having this much fun every day. It seems so stupid that we had to ration it to the last one. I'm sorry.'

'Lily, it's me who should be saying sorry for letting myself get all mushy over that overripe cheese board. What was he called again? I don't think I can even recall his name.'

'Monsieur le stinky Camembert?'

'Ha ha.'

Promenading

We walked along the promenade down by the sea. The sun was setting, turning the sky into a mirage of oranges, lemons, purples and pinks.

'Hey, Mum, who let your wardrobe at the sky?'

'You're right – I think I've got a dress just like that.' She turned around and laughed prettily, her arm linked with Brett's, grinning from ear to ear.

'The place should be just here,' he said. 'The Rue de Holland.'

'What are we looking for?'

'La Grand Hotel Ville de France. It's where Matisse used to stay and paint in the eighteen-hundreds.'

'My mum's got the book, the paintings with the screens and the palm trees and the model.' The thought of telling Mum that I'd been there, stood where Matisse had, maybe even sat on his chair, suddenly made me inexplicably excited.

'It's what first made your mother and me want to come to Tangier – seeing it in *The Sheltering Sky*, the film by Bertolucci, from a book by Paul Bowles. It was years ago,' Maya's dad said.

'It should be just here,' her mum replied.

We were standing outside a large, dilapidated building that was falling to pieces. The windows were boarded up, the paint peeling; an old chrome restaurant sign had its glass smashed, the menu had disintegrated, and the door was bolted.

'Dad,' Maya said. 'It is here. The sign's above your head.'

I waited for a row, but nothing came.

'Never mind, honey. It was a nice walk.' Maya's mum kissed her husband and we walked on to the restaurant, amongst the parading locals in the fading light and the chill of an evening wind.

'Ah, see.' I nudged Maya and nodded my head towards her parents snuggling. 'There is such a thing as "true love".'

'Yuck! That's disgusting. Old people shouldn't be allowed to do that in public. Mum, Dad, no PDA! Respect the Muslim culture.'

3rd January – Time to Go Home

Everything seemed to go in fast-motion from the

moment we got up, to me calling Mum, to the point we'd got into the aeroplane. Suddenly the adventure, our magical mystery tour of Morocco, was over and we were back in our seats flying high above and away from that beautiful and exotic country. François and Olivier were not, thankfully, on the trip back – they were staying a few more days. However, there was a rather nice-looking English boy who smiled at Maya and me on the plane.

'You can have him,' she said. 'He's yours.'

'No, absolutely not. I insist, he's all yours.'

We looked at each other and laughed. The poor boy looked totally bemused.

CHAPTER TEN

Catching Up and Backing Down

3rd January – Worse than a Camel Bite

'Do you not understand what I said?' Mum's face was bright red and she was screaming at all of us. Bay joined in as usual by bursting into Jedi-knight tears in his brown jellaba. Poppy rolled her eyes at me. I tried to imagine myself back in a blue-skied Tangier.

I'd only been in Battersea for an hour and already I was trying to pretend to be walking down the Place de la France past the cafés at sunset again, or looking at the waves crashing together at the Cap Spartel lighthouse. I was trying my hardest, but Mum looked so deranged she reminded me of a sick-faced painting of Medusa on the wall at Art Club, her hair sticking out like snakes. I don't think I'm going to give her her present if she keeps this up.

'Suzi is pregnant. Do you know what that means? Your father is having another child, and it's not you.'

'We understand. We're not Martians. Look, it happens, Mum,' said Poppy, wandering off into the kitchen and putting the kettle on. Bay got bored and followed her in. There was much about Bay in his over-large jellaba that reminded me of a spaniel.

'But why's it happening to us? To me? Why?'

It all made sense to me now. Poor Dad was probably in shock at Christmas – that's why he behaved so badly. And I had noticed the amount Suzi ate for dinner. I wondered if she was eating for triplets? Imagine what Dad would say about that! I quite liked the idea of a new baby; at least Bay would have a chance to see how it was not being the youngest of the family any more, and that could only be good for him.

'I knew this would happen. It was inevitable, from the very beginning.' Mum was miserable with self pity, and vile with loathing. Was I like this last week? Please don't say I'm going to turn into my mum. You're supposed to turn into your mum and marry your dad when you grow up – what a revolting idea! And then she changed track again, her voice softening to a mad sort of sweetness, or a sweet sort of madness. 'So, I've invited them both to dinner to celebrate and welcome you both back, Lily and Poppy. It'll make up for the Christmas fiasco. It'll be nice.'

'Who are you trying to convince? It'll be bedlam,' said Poppy, coming back in. 'Mum, they've told us at school a bit about the change of life, mood swings, flushes. So are you, like, having your menopause? Do you think you should go and see the doctor for a check up?'

'No, I am not! Don't be so bloody cheeky, Poppy.'

'It was just a thought, honestly. No need to get upset.'

'You do have a lot of mood swings, Mum. Maybe your period's due,' I said.

'What is it with you children diagnosing me? It's not even as if you're keen on science. All I'm asking is that you help me make the supper and tidy up a bit this afternoon, before Dad and Suzi come over. I'm the adult here. All right?'

'Are you sure, Mum?' Poppy asked.

Before she had a chance to answer, I yelled out, 'Just off to see Bea.' As I ran for the front door I stopped, did an about-turn and went back to kiss her. 'Don't worry, little Mama, it'll all be OK. I'll be back later to help and then it'll be fine, just you see.' And I smiled at her to try and give her some hope.

'Oh Lily, it's lovely to have you back. Come here for a hug.' And before I had a choice in the matter, she'd practically squeezed the living daylights out of me. Why are mums so odd?

I bet she *is* starting the menopause.

Bea to the Rescue

'I feel odd, very odd,' I said to Bea.

'Why? Are you starting the menopause, too?'

'No, silly.'

'I'm not surprised. I'd feel odd if my dad had a baby.'

'No, I mean I feel odd because I still feel like I'm in Morocco, but clearly I'm not.'

'Sherpas in Mongolia say it takes months for your spirit to catch up with you when you fly. I'm never going to be a pilot or an air steward – you'd lose your spirit in the first month probably and never get it back.'

'Bea, you're very practical and interesting, but what I meant was, I was looking forward to coming home, but it's worse than ever before. And if all that wasn't bad enough, I have to apologise to you, face to face, even though you're looking all loved up and happy with Billy. I have to say sorry for being such a mean old cow in Norfolk when we went on holiday at half-term to Blake's. I now officially know how it feels to be the gooseberry, and I'm sorry.'

'Apology accepted, but what happened? Don't tell me Maya really truly got a boyfriend? I don't believe it!' she said theatrically. It seemed that being happy had actually made her funnier and prettier. Deeply unfair.

'Oh, you will when I tell you the story. Anyway, I told you in the email – he was called François and then I thought I'd fallen for him, too.'

'Yes, but I thought that was a joke. Oh, goody! There's a whole story! I mean boys and Maya? Let's make a nice cup of tea and dunk in some chocolate digestives. Bet they didn't have anything as nice as that in Morocco.' We went into her kitchen, made tea and got out the biscuit tin. 'The food and all those sheep's bits must have been awful. Did the sheep look at you whilst you were eating it?' Back in her room, she offered me the biccies.

'What are you talking about? Thanks, Bea, you're the best,' I said. 'You know, however glamorous and gorgeous it was in Morocco, nothing beats this, being here in your den, dunking biscuits into cups of tea and yapping the afternoon away. You know?'

'Yup, I know just what you mean. Do you think it would be nicer if we tidied up, though?'

'Bea, how do you always get me to tidy up your room?'

Starting a Clean Page

Dear Diary,
When I read back over all the stuff that I wrote in you over Christmas, I sound like the moaniest misery in the world and I know that's not true. So, I'm finishing you here and deserting you for the lovely brand new diary that Mum gave

me and I forgot to take to Morocco. Mum is clearly insane,
but I love her.
A bientôt – *Lily XXX*

I shut the book, locked it, and put it at the back of my wardrobe with the rest of my old diaries.

I opened my new diary – which I hadn't taken to Morocco – and was just smelling the clean pages and wondering if I could bear to spoil their immaculate white blankness and sully them with inconsequential rubbish and the smelly leftovers of my life, when I had an idea – I would start the first page with a pledge, since I was out of the country on January the first; a pledge to govern the rest of the year.

Dear Diary,
With you as my witness, I shall never be:
a) jealous,
b) nasty,
c) purposefully malicious, or
d) downright mean again.
From this day forward I shall be kind and generous, loving
and sharing. I will help Mum, and be generally mature and
sweet to the world, and NOT lose it, either. How hard can it
be? I'm a mature and intelligent girl of fourteen, practically
grown up and living in Paris (not quite yet but it's only a hop

and a skip away) so I will not lose:
   a) my sense of humour
   b) my temper
   c) my lip-gloss
   d) my eye pencil.
   I shall always endeavour . . .

I was clearly immersed in my great literary work. 'Endeavour' was a very good word to use, but what was I going to endeavour to do? I wondered what it was in French? This could be the most fascinating document for a whole future generation of historians and scholars when they are researching my early life in years to come . . . and then I heard a rustle. I looked up, but couldn't see anything. I figured I must have imagined it, but I didn't imagine Mum shouting up from the kitchen, 'Lily, darling, can you please, for the twentieth time, come and help with the dinner? Your father will be here in fifteen minutes.'

I knew she was serious when she said 'father'.

I shouted back, 'Do I have to?' Why bother with intercoms when we all have Lovitt family foghorn-screechers for voices? Most of our conversations carry on with us being in separate rooms, and sometimes on separate floors. 'I'm trying to finish some work in time for school,' I continued. Little white lie, but all writing is good practice for school.

'You liar,' shouted my sister, jumping out from behind the wardrobe door. 'You're just filling your diarrhoea with rubbish.'

'What are you doing in here, Poppy?'

'Borrowing your jacket with the funny sleeves – this one,' she said, grabbing it.

'No, you can't, bug off. And why do you think that you can come into my room whenever you like, creeping in here to steal my stuff, thinking I don't notice?'

'Well you haven't noticed Bay at your dressing table drawing on your mirror. I don't know why you have to be so mean – you've just had a great holiday. Chill out, sis.'

I could write a book filled with the reasons I hate my sister. Calling me 'sis' is just one.

'Oh Bay, that was my favourite lip-gloss. And what have you done to my eye pencil?' At this point Bay stuck out his tongue and did a big, fat, wet, farty raspberry noise and burst into hilarious giggles, running around by himself in a circle. 'That's it – give me the jellaba back. You're too naughty for presents. Bay!'

'No, mine.'

'Give it back now,' I commanded furiously.

And then his lower lip started to tremble as he clung to his Moroccan fancy dress, and fat tears, too big for his eyes, dribbled down his face.

'What's all the noise about, kids?' Mum shouted up.

'Don't be so mean, Lily. What's the matter with you?' Poppy went and cuddled Bay. 'Shhh, baby, it's all right. Lily's just a big, fat meany.'

I turned away and ran downstairs to Mum.

'Mum, Poppy and Bay are being mean to me. Poppy says there's something wrong with me. Do you think there is? I don't know what's wrong with me.'

'No, not wrong, you're just a normal fourteen-year-old girl.'

'But Mum, you don't understand. I can't control anything. Maybe I'm having my menopause? One moment I'm promising stuff in my diary, like to always be nice and not to lose my temper with Bay or Poppy and the next, I'm losing it. It's not normal.'

'It is for a Lily. You've got hormones rushing around you. You can't expect to be normal.'

'So, you still love me?'

'Of course I do, don't be such a silly goose.'

'Do you think Dad does? I mean, will he still, even with a new baby? I had a premonition that this was going to happen, and that he won't talk to us any more.'

'Of course he'll talk to you and love you. You are his one and only Lily. God forbid the world having to cope with another. Now will you lay the table for me, before they arrive?'

'You know, Mum, I've decided that at half-term I'd just

like to stay at home for the whole holiday, explore London and be with my mates. Imagine the fun we could get up to in this our own wonderful city. Do you think London is the best city in the world? I think it might be, when you think about everything.'

'I shudder to imagine the fun you might have. But Tangier was great, wasn't it?'

'Yes, but Mum, though families can be good for you, I've decided other people's should only be taken in small doses, like medicine. Besides, flying unnecessarily is very bad for global warming and we've got to take care of this planet. If we don't, who will? We can't leave it to the politicians or boys. Besides who needs boys when you have friends?'

'I don't quite understand what you're saying, but if it makes sense to you, who am I to doubt it?'

I thought for a moment and then said, 'By the way, Mum, what's going to happen to you and Mr Taylor? I mean Pat. Did you make it up? You know I don't mind if you like him.'

I felt safe saying it, now that she had already told me it was off, but you could never be sure with Mum – one day this, one day that.

'Nothing. I think he was just a tad too immature for our family. It seems for us Lovitt ladies, Christmas wasn't so lucky with love.'

'Poppy's still got Nick.'

'Oh, didn't you get my email? Nick dumped her when they went away. She had to come home on the train alone.'

'Oh no, poor Poppy. I've been so . . . well, I'm not going to be mean to her any more. That is, as long as she isn't mean to me first. Poor Poppy! She really liked Nick, and he was sick over my shoes and even I still liked him. Poppy, you can borrow my jacket,' I shouted upstairs.

'Already have,' she shouted back. Typical.

'Anyway, as you always say, Lily, why would I need a boyfriend with all you kids to deal with and my painting exhibition coming up?'

'You know, Mum, you might not be as rich or as glamorous as Maya's mum, Nancy, but I think you're a much nicer, funnier person, and you are quite good-looking for your age. And don't you worry, you can leave it to me – if it's the last thing I do, I'm going to find you a nice boyfriend. Might even be a husband. Think of the fun we can have on the internet. I bet there are loads of old mingers up there.'

'There goes the doorbell, Lily.'

'Don't worry, I'll get it.'

'And Lily, what do you mean, "old mingers"? I wonder if Madonna wants to adopt some older British children for her multicultural family.'

I pretended not to hear. 'What were you saying, Mum? Dad and Suzi are here,' I screamed out, and Poppy and Bay came rushing down.

I really was back home in the comfort of my family, however mad they were. Strange, but I'd really miss them if I lived in Paris.

Really, no, really I would – really, truly, deeply, and definitely madly.

The Lilicionary

Translations of some of my French phrases :

à bientôt – see you
aussi – also
beaucoup – a lot
bien – good; well
bien sûr – of course
bijoux – jewellery
ça va? – how are you?
c'est comme ça – so it goes (lit. It's like that)
c'est dégueulasse – it's disgusting
c'est la vie – that's life
chameaux – camels
charmant – charming; delightful
chaussures – shoes
chemise – shirt
chérie – dear
choix – choice
cochon – pig
combien ? – how much?
comment allez vous? – how are you? (lit. How are you going?)
comprends? – understand?
cordons de la burse – purse strings
curieux – curious

coeur – heart

délicat – delicate

derrière – bottom

dirham – a dirham (Moroccan currency)

dix – ten

dix-sept – seventeen

douze – twelve

en français – in French

enfants – children

envoûter – to bewitch

espionnage – espionage, spying

fermer la bouche – to close the mouth

filles – girls

fleur – flower

j'aime t'achète culotte – I like to buy pants

je me suis baigné dans le Poème De la Mer –
    I have bathed in the poem of the sea

je ne sais pas – I don't know

je ne sais quoi – 'a certain something'

je parle français – I speak French

je pense – I think

je suis désolée – I am sorry

je t'adore – I adore you

jeune – young

joie de vivre – joy of living

joyeux – joyful/cheery

lentement – slowly

livre – book

mais – but

merci – thank you

mille – thousand

millefeuille – custard pastry (lit. thousand sheets)

mon Dieu! – my God!

ne pas – not

non – no

ne seulement pas – not just

Noël – Christmas

nous sommes arrivés – we have arrived

parapluie – umbrella

pardon – sorry

parfait – perfect

pas de quoi – don't mention it

pas moins que – not less than

petit – small/little

petit-déjeuner – breakfast

petit peu – a little bit

peut-être – perhaps

porte-monnaie – purse/wallet

pour – for

prix – price

quelle surprise – what a surprise

qui est . . . ? – who is . . . ?

quoi? – what?
raison d'être – reason of being
rien – nothing
sabre – sword
toi – you
toqué – batty
tout – everything
treize – thirteen
très – very
trois – three
trop – too
tu es – you are
vite – quick
zut alors! – oh my goodness!

Other books in the *Life and Loves of Lily* series:

Sophie Parkin

Lily is in for a dire three weeks, stranded in the Lake District at CampHappy with no phone and no friends. But she's independent and determined, and at least there's email and a welcome break from her completely mad family – a mother who hugs trees, a father whose girlfriend is closer to Lily's age than her mum's, a demanding older sister, and a small, adorable and infuriating brother. So camp can't be too bad, can it?

A funny, frank and fresh take on learning to love others, yourself and some very cute boys. Accepting the bonkers behaviour of the rest of Earth's inhabitants might be hard, but '*Plus ça change!*', as Lily would say.
It's not all about learning to camp, you know . . .

Mad, Rich, and Famous

Sophie Parkin

Best friends and boyfriends don't always mix!

When Lily's invited to stay with her new boyfriend, she brings her best mate Bea along as well. She can't wait to see the gorgeous Blake again and it's the perfect opportunity to escape from her impossible family.

But Lily's life is never easy. Blake turns out to live on a spooky country estate with his truly terrifying parents – and Lily's not even sure she likes him any more. However it's Bea who turns out to be the real problem . . . *Zut alors!*

☆

www.piccadillypress.co.uk

☆ The latest news on forthcoming books

☆ Chapter previews

☆ Author biographies

☆ Fun quizzes

☆ Reader reviews

☆ Competitions and fab prizes

☆ Book features and cool downloads

☆ And much, much more . . .

Log on and check it out!

Piccadilly Press

☆